THE LIGHT OF THE ÉLAN VITAL

VITAL

SOUL SEARCHING BOOK 1

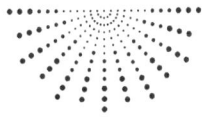

JEN TYES

ISBN-13: 978-1-7337469-0-8

ISBN-10: 1-7337469-0-0

Editing by Crow Editing

Book cover design by Vibrant Design

Printed in the United States of America

Visit www.jentyes.com

For all the artists of the world. Your mind creates beauty so never let anyone tell you that your creations are unworthy of admiration.

DEFINITIONS

Emez (n.) - A planet that has been in existence since the dawn of time, though their known history only dates back a few centuries. There is no record of the world before the current inhabitants. Emez has two locations— The *Isle of Vaehte* and *The Beneath*.

The Isle of Vaehte (n.) - An inhabitable utopian place, also known as *The Isle*, which floats in the Emez atmosphere using positive energy, like oxygen, to survive. When the positive, pure energy is unbalanced, the fate and lives of the Vaehte people are at stake (*see The Isle Energy*).

The Isle Energy (n.) - The energy is what gives the Vaehte people long and beautiful lives. Everyone has a recycle date that is dependent on the purity of the energy. The more positive and pure the energy, the longer one lives. When one person expires, another person is born, surging the Isle with the purest of energy.

The Beneath (n.) - The Beneath is below The Isle. Most believe that the Beneath was once a place where people lived.

It is now a prison for those who cannot maintain life on the Isle. The Beneath is neither positive nor negative. Since the Beneath accepts all types of energy, it was not long after the first fallen fell that it began to grow and thrive. The fallen being fuel to the Beneath, and allowing it to flourish. It is forbidden for any Vaehte person on the Isle to travel to the Beneath. It is easy to get into, but almost impossible to leave, due to the attractiveness of neutral energy. In the last century, the Beneath has been growing out of proportion and the distance between the Beneath and the Isle is decreasing. The Isle of Vaehte is dying, along with the Vaehte people. If the two worlds touch, the dark energy from the Beneath will consume the Isle and make it dark and uninhabitable for the Vaehte people. They will cease to exist.

Vaehte (n.) - These are the inhabitants of The Isle. They have human features and skin the color of Bronze. They have sophisticated brains; having psychic and empathic abilities. They sense emotions and changes in mood, and can also alter moods and emotions. They can treat any illness and heal each other with just a thought. They also use that superior psychic power to teleport by thought.

The Fallen (n.) - They are the Vaehte people who have fallen from grace. The Fallen corrupt the positive, pure flow of energy, and no longer contribute to the survival of the Isle. They are then banished to the Beneath.

The Hight Appointed (n.) - The Isle is governed by a group called the High Appointed. The High Appointed control and manage the balance and they answer to the Grand Father. They keep records of all born and those who have expired. They dictate births and assist with all new and expired life force energies.

The Grand Father (n.) - The Grand Father is the equivalent to royalty. Although he does not make all the decisions, he allows his counsel, the High Appointed, to present their decisions for his sign off. He is a warrior and the voice and face of the High Appointed.

The prophecy (n.) - Legend states there is a prophecy that says there will be balance once again. Every one of Emez knows of the prophecy and knows that fulfilling it is the key to replenishing the pure energy. Over the years, the prophecy's content has been mistranslated and skewed. According to legend, those mentioned in the prophecy know the true translation and will bring about unity and balance.

PART I
IT BEGAN WITH A DREAM

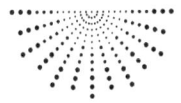

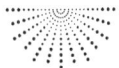

"*M*ommy!! Mommy!" Keera screams as she sits straight up in her bed, bringing her feet to her chest, hugging them tightly.

She takes a look around the room, expecting something to jump out at her from the dark. There is no movement, and only the sound of breathing can be heard. Just as she is about to cry out again, the door opens. Her mother, Susan, peers in, clutching her chest with horror written on her face. She looks down at her daughter's small frame and her expression softens. She slides into the twin bed with Keera and wraps her arms around her. "They're dying! They're dying!" Her voice is filled with anguish as she melts into her mother. She visibly shakes with fear in her mother's arms, whispering, "They're dying, they're dying. They need the sun, they need the light. Where is the light?" Keera looks wildly about the room, scrunching her face. Her mother coos as she begins to rock. "Hush, Hush, sweetie. It was just a bad dream."

Keera relaxes in her mother's arms and begins shaking her

head and crying, before trying to force words out, "Mommy, it was real. It was so real." Susan continues to rock, and caress her hair. They rock until the sobs become small hiccups. She pulls Keera slightly away so that she can look into her eyes.

She speaks as softly and lovingly as possible, "Kee, do you want to tell me what you saw? Would that help you get back to sleep?" Keera loves when her mother uses her pet name. It is filled with so much love that she feels safe at that moment. She takes a deep breath and thinks back to her dream. Her heart begins to beat erratically. "Mommy, it was so scary." Fresh tears begin to form in her eyes as a look of realization crosses her face. "The sunlight was going down and people were dying." Keera's sentence ends hoarsely as she tries to keep the tears from falling.

Susan kisses Keera on her forehead, hoping that her kiss will erase the trauma from the dream. They sit in silence for a while. "Baby, look around." She hopes she can ease Keera's pain by showing her things from her perspective.

Keera glances slightly around the room, noticing that her two older sisters, Mara and Thena, are still sound asleep. She looks up at her mom who looks down and gives her a smile. "See, everything is fine. The sun is down, but it will rise again in the morning. For now, we have the moon to light the way."

Keera looks to the window and sees the moon shining through, giving off the brightest white light, making her relax more. Her mother slips out of the bed. "Now lay down and try and get some sleep." Keera lies down while her mother tucks her in. She moves a lock of hair from Keera's face before planting a kiss on her brow. Susan retreats toward the door, turning to smile and blow a kiss before slowly closing the door. Thinking better of fully closing the door, she opens the door just a crack, in case Keera calls out again before daybreak. Keera looks around once more, wishing her mother would come back into the room, before closing her eyes. She thinks of her mother as she drifts away toward a dreamless sleep.

CHAPTER TWO

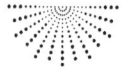

The nights following the first dream were filled with more dreams. Unlike the first night, Keera did not call out to her mother. The dreams were not all the same and since that first dream, Keera always felt a calming sensation come over her whenever she was afraid. It was as if the strength of her name from her mother's lips followed her in the dreams and made her feel safe. After about three week of dreaming of this far-off land, Keera began to see figures in the distance. They were never close up, but she could tell they were different. In her good dreams, these people, the light people, filled her with the happiest feelings. She wanted to stay with them because it felt so right. On nights when she had horrible dreams of darkness, she would close her eyes tight and think of her mother, which always brought a sense of calm flowing through her.

One night, while dreaming of the light people, she noticed one of them appeared more defined than the others. This particular light person seemed to be looking directly at her.

She squinted her eyes to look closer, but could only make out the figure, surrounded by light. Deep down, Keera knew that this figure was important and it was, in fact, looking at her. This intrigued Keera. As she tried to make out more of the figure's features, the light around it began to grow, which filled Keera with fear. The fear she felt was not like what she felt when the darkness was surrounding her, but more like the fear of not understanding what was happening in her dreams. She quickly closed her eyes and thought about her mother.

She imagined her mother calling her name in the loving way she does and began to feel the fear ebb. Keera continued to focus her thoughts on her mother, when she heard someone call her name. She opened her eyes and looked around. There was no one there; just bright light all around. The light continued to spread and brighten, until Keera had to close her eyes but even with her eyes closed, the light penetrated her whole body, shocking Keera awake in her bed. She lay in the silence, expecting something or someone to stir, but the night remained calm and quiet. She eventually fell back into a dreamless sleep.

The next morning, Keera was roused from her sleep by her name being yelled from somewhere in the house. It was her mother calling from, most likely, the kitchen. Finally, Keera remembered it was a school day and if she's being called, she was probably running late. She sat up and noticed that Thena and Mara were no longer in their beds. She listened for the bathroom sink. The water wasn't running. Keera realized that she was running extremely late. Just as she was jumping out of bed, her mother was at the door, entering the room. "Breakfast is getting cold, so dress quickly and don't forget to brush your teeth."

Her mother turned to leave and she heard her say, *Goodness, I hope she's not getting sick.* Her father, Thena and Mara's stepdad, had left them when she was three, so her mother had to go back to work earlier than she had planned to care for them. Keera knew that her mom didn't like taking time out of work to care for her or one of her sisters. Without her dad being there with them, she noticed her mom was extremely tired from work most days.

Before her mother closed the door, Keera reassured her, "I feel fine, mommy. I was just sleeping deep." Her mother turned back with a bewildered look, realizing that her little girl had just responded to something she was thinking to herself. She opened her mouth, then closed it as Keera ran to the adjoining bathroom to get ready for school. She slowly backed out of the room, closing the door, unsure of how to respond to what had just happened. Life was beginning to take a strange turn.

CHAPTER THREE

*T*he changes in Keera were subtle, at first. She began picking up on her mother's thoughts, which was causing Susan some discomfort and, surprisingly, a lot of curiosity. She didn't know if she should just accept Keera's new abilities, or take her to a doctor for a possible brain tumor. Keera did not appear any different, except that she could now read her mother's thoughts. Susan also had the nagging feeling that she should explore Keera's abilities, to understand them. Something like this would normally have Susan running to the nearest hospital, but the nagging curiosity was extremely strong, so she decided to give in and try to understand what had changed in her daughter.

Keera also began to notice that things had changed between her and her mom. She began to instinctively know her mother's needs, before her mother would speak. Keera also noticed that her mother was acting weird. She was more interested in how Keera was feeling, and would constantly ask random questions. It made Keera feel good, knowing that her mother was spending so much more time with her. But Keera began to notice Thena and Mara becoming more aware of the attention that she was getting from their mother. They weren't mad at Keera, like other siblings would be. They had always protected her, since her dad left. They knew how it felt to not have a father around, so they tried their hardest to be there for her. It was like they felt they had to grow up faster to make up for the absence of a father figure. Though Keera was only six, she was very aware of what was going on within their family. Keera would hear them think sad thoughts. Most of the time, they were missing their mother's attention. To Keera's appreciation, they never shunned her for receiving the attention. Keera began to notice her dreams were surrounded by darkness once again. She was no longer scared of the dreams because she took the love of her mother with her. Keera felt like the turn in the dreams was related to the imbalance of affection her sisters felt in her waking life. Once Keera realized her dreams were connected to her waking life, she made sure they were included more, without making Susan feel bad for being so singularly focused. Keera realized that she had to protect her sisters, just as they protect her, even if they were four and six years older. They were a family, and all they had in the world. With this new resolve, everyone was happy, and the light dreams returned.

As she got closer to her mom through thought, and the emotional balance within their household returned, her light dreams began to get more clear. Instead of just seeing bright light figures, she was starting to see the figures as what she thought were male or female. There was a glow surrounding their forms, and their skin was unlike anything she had ever seen. Their skin was a shiny brown, or bronze, that looked like it moved. It was so beautiful and mesmerizing.

Keera wondered what it all meant. One of the figures, a man, began to approach her. His long jet-black hair swayed behind him as he floated, yes floated, her way. With every "step" closer, she felt a greater sense of calm. When he was finally within a few feet of Keera, she noticed the beautiful golden swirls of his eyes. She smiled up at his towering frame and tentatively said hi. *Hello, Keera.* The words were spoken without him moving his mouth. He saw that Keera was in a bit of shock, so he spoke using his voice, "I have been looking forward to meeting you for a long time. Tell me, do you know who I am?" His voice was a force in itself, so strong and commanding. Keera shook her head slowly, still in shock. "My name is Terafey. I am the Grand Father. You are currently amongst the Vaehte people — or who you call the light people."

Keera had never told anyone about her dreams, or of the light people she saw in them. This new Grand Father was beginning to amaze her. Grand Father chuckled when he noticed the look of surprise across Keera's face, then continued on, "You see that I can speak to you without using my mouth, but you can hear it in your mind?" He pointed to his temple as Keera nodded her head. "You can do it, too!"

Keera stood there a moment, thinking on what the Grand Father said. She questioned if he was real, if this was real, and if she would really be able to speak to people without moving her mouth. Before she could respond, the light began to brighten and the figures began to disappear within the glow. Before the bright lights caused Keera totally blindness, Grand Father spoke in her mind, one last time, *We'll meet again, young Keera.*

CHAPTER FOUR

*K*eera began looking forward to bedtime. This did not disturb her mother, because after long days at work, she welcomed the no-fuss bedtime routine, and the silence that followed. As Keera prepared for bed, her body buzzed with excitement. Grand Father has been a beacon, a pure light, and the piece that she had been missing in her waking life.

With each dream, Keera learned more and more about the light people and their world. Grand Father would show Keera different and new things in his world, that she would never find on Earth. He would teach her many things that she could do using her mind, and tonight, she planned to show him her skills.

Keera ran over to Thena and Mara's beds and gave them big hugs. "Good night!" she shouted as she ran back over to her side of the room and hopped into bed. Mara gave Thena a raised eyebrow, as if to question Keera's actions and Thena answered with a shoulder shrug. They both looked over at

Keera and watched her tuck herself in and settle into bed, without waiting for Susan to come in and say good night.

Susan walked in a few minutes later to complete the nightly routine, stopping short at Keera's bed. She looked over at Thena and Mara, who gave their mother shoulder shrugs before climbing into their own beds for the night. Susan shakes her head as she walked over to say good night to Thena and Mara. Whispering, she asked them if Keera was okay. Mara answered, "I guess. maybe she's excited for school tomorrow." Their mother agreed before bending over to give Mara a kiss good night. She turned to Thena, bopped her on the nose and made a 'boop' sound. "Good night, honey," she said, bending over to give Thena a kiss.

She stood up and turned so that both girls could see her. She draws a heart in the air with her index fingers, each making one side of a heart, then pointed to both girls. Thena and Mara smiled and each drew a half of one heart, followed by pointing to Susan. They settled into bed and closed their eyes. Susan walked toward the door, she leaned down to give Keera a kiss on her brow before exiting their bedroom.

Sleep finds Keera easily and takes her to the land of the light people. She knows where to find Grand Father and makes her way toward the garden she knows he'll be in. He enjoys being out with nature, he says it clears his mind and brings him closer to peace. As Keera approaches the garden, she can see Grand Father sitting in a meditative position. She stops short of entering the garden, to gather her confidence to greet him. She closes her eyes, takes a deep breath, and steadies her heart. She focuses on Grand Father, sensing his presence ahead of her, and speaks to him telepathically, *Hello*

Grand Father. Keera opens her eyes, expecting to see Grand Father respond to her words, but he does not move or acknowledge her presence. She thought that she had made a mistake so she tries again, more timidly this time. *Hello.* She opens her eyes, but still there is no acknowledgement. She keeps her eyes open and sends another greeting, *Hello?* Grand Father still makes no move to acknowledge Keera's words. Keera feels that she has worked really hard to learn from Grand Father. She even tried with her mother. She would call her mother, using telepathy, while hiding around the corner, and watch her mother turn around, expecting to see her standing behind her.

She knows that she can do it and can not understand why it is not working in her dream. Disappointment begins to seep through and, without meaning to, Keera put her all into sending a telepathic message to Grand Father. *TERAFEY!* Grand Father brought his hands to his head and fell over into the fetal position. Keera saw what she had done and ran over to help him. Keera began to cry and ask him not to hurt, while apologizing simultaneously. Without knowing, Keera was using her energy to bring peace to Grand Father.

He slowly took his hands away from his ears and opened his eyes to take notice of Keera. He was amazed at what she was able to do. Grand Father knew Keera had arrived, and knew that she was eager to try her new skills, so he waited. He pretended he didn't know she was there. He wanted to acknowledge her only once he heard her in his mind. It was a difficult task, and he knew she could do it. It was a lesson that Keera needed to see through, without him, and he respected the passion in her young heart. He did not expect the strength in her message. Not only did she successfully speak telepathically, she also manipulated her energy, which is something he had yet to teach her. He wanted to make sure she knew she did not do anything wrong, so he made every attempt to soothe her. He sent her some calming energy, as he'd done so often in other dreams, "Keera, I am here. I am fine. You did nothing wrong. I am very proud of you."

Keera continued crying. Her tears were beginning to affect the people and plants around them, and Grand Father knew he had to fix it. "Keera, look around." He put his hand to Keera's chin and gently lifted her head, so that she could look out. Keera opened her eyes and looked around. Her eyes became very large when she saw what was happening. People were standing around, watching her cry over the Grand Father, who was, to her surprise, unharmed by what happened. Keera noticed that the people were not as bright as they were when she had arrived. She looked around more and noticed the flowers were less erect and looked sad. Keera's eyes grew big when she realized that it was her that was the cause of this disaster, "This is my fault." Keera looked down at her hands in her lap and just stared at them. Grand Father rose from the ground and held his hands out for Keera to take them and stand up. Once standing, Grand Father spoke, "What you see is the effect of your sadness. We are affected by energy and emotions. But remember, this is only a dream. You have not hurt anyone." Keera looked up at Grand Father with confusion, then sadness. Grand Father understood her feelings, and knew what she was thinking. "Keera, I am very real and my people, the Vaehte people, are real but what you see here is a dream version of our very real world. You are very special, did you know that?" Keera shook her head. "Well, you are very special and you do not have to worry, because I am here and I will never leave you."

Keera is unsure, but she feels like Grand Father has known her all her life. He knew that her father had left when she was three; he knew that she missed her dad but could barely remember anything about him. He knew that she worried about Thena and Mara because they always felt the need to take care of her, when they should just be kids. With anything Keera and Grand Father discuss, he always finds a way to calm her worry. Her sadness began to clear and the light was becoming bright. Keera wished that he was with her every day and just as the thought passed through her mind, the light surrounding them began to intensify and blind her. She began to panic, because she wasn't ready for her time with Grand Father to end. The light became too bright and the dream started to fade. *You are special. Keep practicing. Until the next time.* Keera woke up to sunlight shining into the room. She smiled and decided that the next time she saw Grand Father, she would greet him telepathically on the first try.

Keera tried unsuccessfully to read her family at breakfast. She had done it before but, for some reason, was having difficulty after what had happened in her dream. Keera slumped down into her chair and felt every ounce of defeat. She felt tears forming in her eyes, then heard Mara's barely-audible voice, "I wish she'd just tell us what's wrong." Keera looked up, but only saw Mara reading her book. Keera tilted her head to the side and continued looking at Mara. *Now she's just staring. What has gotten into her?* A spark of realization hit Keera when she heard the whisper of Mara's thoughts. She slowly smiled. I still got it, she thought to herself and continued with her meal.

At home, Keera felt as special as Grand Father said she was, but at school, nothing made her feel special. She did not have many friends and things were made worse because she was also great with her school work. Keera knew the kids at school didn't believe she was special. The kids were cruel but today, Keera didn't mind that she was isolated at school. She would use this to practice her telepathy, and get stronger, so that she could show Grand Father that she is every bit as special as he said she is.

The school day began as any school day begins for Keera; Susan put her on the bus before driving into work. Keera hates riding the bus, but because of their mother's work schedule, she and her sisters take the bus to school. Every morning, the four of them wait at the bus stop together. They fill the time with jokes, laughter, and pure happiness. Thena and Mara's bus came first. Since they were older, and went to the middle school in town, Keera felt further loneliness in school. After waving good bye and watching their bus drive away, the rest of the wait at the bus stop always filled Keera with dread. Though she loves school for the new things that she learns, she wishes that the kids were nicer to her.

Keera goes directly to her classroom, once she arrives at school. She walks with her head down, so that she can only see a few steps in front of her, so as not to bump into anyone. She knows the way to her classroom with her eyes closed, but the kids at school were unpredictable and she would rather not draw attention her way by bumping into anyone.

She arrives at her classroom and takes her assigned seat.

She thinks about who she would try to read and learn more about. Keera thought about reading her teacher, but thinks better of it because any glimpse into how a teacher feels about a student would forever change her. She is looking from desk to desk, imagining the person who sits there, when a boy named Patrick entered the room. Keera blushes. Patrick is the smartest and nicest boy in class. He tells jokes and gets in trouble, but he has a way of talking himself out of a trip to the principal's office.

Patrick's desk is right next to Keera's desk. As she watches him enter the room and make his way to his desk, Keera decides that he would be perfect to try and get to know better. Trying to convince herself that she picked him because he is nice to her, Keera finds herself staring at him from her seat. He has black curly hair and a chocolate skin complexion that reminds Keera of a Hershey kiss. There is no age restriction when it comes to recognizing beauty and attraction. Keera isn't the only one who notices. Today, Keera finds out that a group of girls in her class took notice of Keera, taking notice of Patrick.

Keera didn't realize that other people were filing into the classroom. Most people ignore her, but for some reason there are three girls who can never seem to act like Keera doesn't exist. Marissa, the leader of the trio, pushed past Keera's desk, knocking her slightly off balance and out of her daydream. In that same moment, Patrick notices Keera looking in his direction, so he smiles and says hello. Keera blushes and whispers a greeting back. Marissa and her friends, Lana and Kendra, laugh as they pass Keera's desk. Keera turns and finds them huddled together and, without reading their thoughts, she already knows they are talking about her.

Throughout the day, this group of girls make fun of Keera; they are nonstop with the teasing. They saw how Keera was looking at Patrick and without knowing the reason for the stare, they assumed, albeit correctly, that she has a crush on Patrick, the most popular boy in class.

When they realize that Keera is not going to give in to their teasing, they take their torture further than Keera has ever witnessed. During lunch, Marissa makes sure that Keera knows who is boss. Most days, Keera eats alone. There are days when a few kids and Keera would eat lunch alone, together, but today is not one of those days. As she sits at the lunch table, eating the provided school lunch, Kendra approaches and sits at the table, across from Keera. Keera looks up and sees Kendra batting her eyes and smiling at her. Keera looks at her with confusion. Kendra says nothing, she just turns her head to her left and points. Apparently she wants Keera to look, so she turns right to see what has Kendra acting so weird. Keera's eyes go wide. She sees Marissa and Lana, sitting with Patrick, huddled together and laughing. Keera tries to straighten her expression, but her mouth drops open when she sees Lana pointing in her direction with her left hand and covering a laugh with her right. She knew in that moment that they went over just to tell him that she liked him. Not knowing how he will react, Keera tries to listen to his thoughts, hoping to hear good news. Clear as day, Keera heard *ewww*. She can see that he hadn't said it aloud and is being nice as he explains that he doesn't like her to Marissa and Lana. They find it hilarious, no matter what he said. It cuts so deeply that she turns back to Kendra, who is still sitting across from her but now laughing. Keera is so embarrassed and hurt that she runs from the lunchroom, ignoring the calls from the teachers and monitors, and hides in the girls' bathroom for the rest of the day.

CHAPTER FIVE

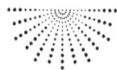

$\mathcal{T}$he guidance counselor had to call her mom to come pick her up from school, noting that Keera was having a difficult time. Susan was quite furious and deeply concerned when she arrived. Keera knew that this was affecting her mother's work day, but just felt that she couldn't carry on with the day. When she was signed out for the day and outside the building, Keera ran to the car, without giving her mother a chance to ask what happened. Susan tried to catch and console her, but Keera ran past her so fast, she didn't get a chance to say anything. Keera had never felt this defeated, alone, and a complete waste of space. She just wanted to cry in her room, alone. She couldn't understand how her mother and sisters loved her. She couldn't fathom what the Grand Father saw in her. Maybe her dreams were a reflection of how she felt her family felt about her, and Terafey was just part of her imagination. Just the thought of that even being a possibility sent Keera spiraling even further down.

When they reached home, Keera ran to her room, slammed the door, and flung herself across her bed. The only sounds heard were the sound of her wails and her mother in the distance, on the telephone, calling in to work. Without notice, every sound, including her cries, disappeared. Keera looked around, thinking that she had lost her hearing. She tested her voice and found that it made no sound. The room slowly disappeared and she began to see this beautiful place. It felt like the epitome of pure happiness, like what she felt around the light people. The emotions she felt about school became insignificant, compared to this new and almost inconceivable joy she felt being here. She closed her eyes to try and absorb the loving energy of this place, when there came a voice. It was the voice of the Grand Father. "Your future is bigger than the problems you face. You are meant for great things and one day you will understand." Keera listened, then asked if he was real. He ignored her question and said that she was strong enough to face the meanest of them all. She felt a blanket of comfort wrap around her body. She closed her eyes to embrace it. He has to be real, she thought. After he spoke, the bedroom began to come into focus. The beautiful place disappeared, but the feeling remained. It wasn't enough to stop Keera's tears but it was enough for her to realize that Marissa and her friends would never hurt her like that again. Keera held onto the feeling of pure happiness and comfort, in expectation that one day she would feel it again.

When Thena and Mara arrived home, Susan prepared them for Keera's well-being. Susan was very worried, as Keera refused to leave the bedroom, and hoped that Thena and Mara could pull what had happened out of Keera so that they can get past it. Susan suspects it had something to do with the kids at school. It would not be the first time that Keera had withdrawn from everyone because some kids at school had bullied her. Susan would march down to the school the next morning and put a stop to it all, for her baby's sake.

Once Susan asked Thena and Mara to comfort and discover the root of her pain, it was Mara that spoke up to Thena, telling her she thought it was the kids at school. So, as they ascended the stairs to their bedroom to soothe Keera, they discussed how they could get the names of those kids from her lips. Thena and Mara both thought Keera was acting strange lately. Mara, being the oldest, knew she didn't deserve how the kids at school were treating her. She and Thena planned to get to the bottom of it and protect their little sister.

Thena peeked into their bedroom, looking in on Keera. She was on her stomach, laying on her bed, reading one of her early reader books. She looked fine, and not at all like what their mother had described to them. Thena backed away from the doorframe and motioned for Mara to look in. Mara peeked into the room, then quickly turned back to Thena, closing the door again.

"What is going on?" Mara threw her arms up wide, looking confused as she asked the question. "Mara, something is definitely wrong, but she looks fine. Maybe she's so upset that she can't even express it." Mara stood a bit straighter, "We have to do something then. Let's go in and just check on her." Thena agreed. Mara opened the door and both girls walked in.

Thena and Mara tentatively approached Keera's bed. They looked down on her for a moment before Thena found her voice. "Umm, Keera, whatcha doing? " Keera turned to face her sisters. She had a great big smile on her face. "Hey! I'm just reading my book." Thena moved to sit on Keera's bed. Mara followed suit before speaking slowly, with concern, "We heard what happened today." Keera's smile turned down, "Oh." She looked down at her hands and began to poke at a scab on her left thumb. Thena looked at Mara, widening her eyes in annoyance. Mara hunched her shoulders and nodded her head toward Keera, telling Thena to speak next. "Are you okay? Keera, you know we are here for you. Please tell us what happened." Thena waited, but Keera just sat there. The silence dragged on until Keera let out a loud exhale. She lifted her head and smiled at her sisters. "There's a group of girls at school that told a boy I liked him, and I was embarrassed. But I now know that I am bigger than that. I may not understand it all now, but one day I will, and what happened today won't matter." Keera lifted her right shoulder as if to say, 'whatever'. Thena looked at Keera and then to Mara, who was looking at Keera, with her mouth hanging open. Thena twisted her face when she realized that she was not going to get any help from Mara, then turned back to Keera, who was looking at her expectantly. "Well, you know you can talk to us about anything. Just give me the word and I will handle those girls," Thena said that last part half-joking and half-serious, which made Keera laugh aloud. "I know, Thena. Thank you for always being there for me." Keera continued giggling as she leaned toward Thena and Mara to give them a group hug. Thena automatically wrapped her right arm around Keera, but it took Mara a moment to break out of her trance before wrapping her left arm around Keera. Per ritual, Keera put her head between her sisters' heads and Thena and Mara intertwined their fingers, meeting behind Keera's back. After the hug broke, Thena and Mara got up from Keera's bed and retreated from the room. Keera laid back on her stomach and continued reading her book.

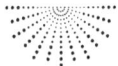

CHAPTER SIX

*K*eera returned to school reluctantly. She was escorted to the school by her mother, which both embarrassed, and filled Keera with pride. The Grand Father had extinguished her feelings about the situation, so Keera no longer felt the pain and sadness that Marissa and her friends had caused. She never wanted them to get in trouble, and less so right now. Susan had insisted that Keera tell her what happened, and then demanded the names of all involved. Keera knew that her mother would not give up until she got the information, so Keera didn't even resist. When Thena and Mara came downstairs after speaking with Keera, they told their mother everything that Keera had said, which made her think that Keera was emotionally scarred by the actions of these kids. Although her words surprised Thena, and more so Mara, Thena didn't think it was scarring but something else; something she could not put her hands on. Mara told her mom that she'd keep a close eye on Keera and that made

Susan feel slightly better, but did not stop her from making a scene at Keera's school.

As Keera sat in the office, while her mother *reasoned* with the principal, she thought about Grand Father. He still amazed her. He knew everything about her, and knew when she needed him before she even thought to call for him. It astonished her that he reached out to her while she was awake. With as much care as he's shown for her, she was beginning to feel just as special as he said she was. She's asked on many occasions to be removed from this school and the answer has always been no, as it will be again. No matter, Keera continued to sit quietly, smiling internally, knowing the kids at school will never get to her again.

Susan walked out of the principal's office and let out a loud exhale. She looked toward Keera and gave her a smile. Keera remained seated as her mother approached and sat in the seat next to her. Susan took Keera's hands in her own, caressing them as if she was about to give her the worst news imaginable. Keera reached out to her mother's mind and tried to read her. *Oh God! Why is this always so hard!?*

Keera wanted to save her mother some anguish so she spoke before her mom could utter a word, "Mom, it's okay. I know I have to stay. The year is almost over. Then I'll get a break." Susan looked at Keera's smiling face and then focused on Keera's eyes. Susan looked, and wondered when her baby girl had become so wise and knew just what to say. As if hearing the thought, Keera's smile widened while pushing herself into her mother for a big hug. The hug lasted longer than normal and before pulling away, Keera whispered, "I love you, mom. Because of you, I am strong." Susan allowed a tear to fall from each of her eyes. She made sure to clear her face before ending their hug. Keera got up and turned to walk to her class. She turned back in time to see her mother mouth, 'I love you, too'.

CHAPTER SEVEN

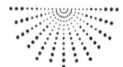

The school year continued without an issue. Keera went back to class after leaving her mother in the school's main office. Marissa and her friends tried to hurt her again, using Patrick as bait, but Keera would not give them a reaction. Every time they would tempt her, she would think about her mother and Terafey, and it was like the bullies were not even in the room. Eventually, they got the hint and moved on to the next person on their list. Keera was once again free to be herself, and practice the skills that would lead her to a great future.

As the school year was coming to an end, so were her dreams. The Grand Father didn't tell her that the dreams would end. They just got shorter, and then far and fewer in between. He had lied, which made Keera very mad. He said he would never leave her and he left, just like her father. At the thought of her father leaving, Keera's anger quickly turned into sadness. How can it be that she is this unloveable? She felt a spark in her heart and instantly wiped that thought away. She had her mother and sisters. She was loveable. This filled her with a resolution. Although Keera was sad, she continued to practice and review everything that the Grand Father had told her. She would not let the disappearance of her dreams stop her from practicing. For whatever reason, she felt deep-down that it was important in some way. She became stronger mentally, and as she mastered what Grand Father had taught her, she yearned for more lessons. She knew that there was more to learn, but without the dreams, there was no one to teach her. Without the Grand Father, Keera knew that there was no one else capable of teaching her what she knows she needs to learn.

The summer arrived quickly and Keera all but forgot about the Grand Father. It felt as if she had lost a father for a second time, and with that, her skills began to suffer. She tried not to dwell on the loss too much. Instead, she did the things that the rest of the kids were doing during summer break. She rode her bike, played with her dolls, went to the community pool, and mostly just had fun. Through play, she let go of the stress of not knowing when she would see Grand Father and became just a child again.

Being like all the other kids, Keera became more confident in herself. It was as if letting go and being a happy child was the key to letting go mentally, which brought out the best in her mental abilities. Keera began to effortlessly hear the thoughts of her sisters and mother. When she would play with other children, she would hear them, as well. Being in public places became a loud experience, so Keera started focusing on individual play, with dolls. With her dolls, she allowed her imagination to run wild, and felt strong without the thoughts of others invading her mind.

As the summer was coming to an end, Keera used her dolls to replay some of her dreams. She felt her dreams fading away more and more, and sadness over the loss of the Grand Father became the center of her world. Mara and Thena would try to console her, but she just didn't think they could understand the loss she felt for a person who did not exist in her waking life and, more recently, did not even exist in her dreams. Her mother had once asked her to confide in her. Susan was very concerned because of Keera's withdrawal from playing with her friends. Keera told her mother that her beautiful dreams stopped coming and were fading away from her memories. Susan told her that she could simply set her dream intentions before going to sleep, and make her dreams be whatever she wanted them to be. Keera wanted to roll her eyes, but refrained from using the common reaction she had recently picked up from Thena. But in that moment, Keera realized that her mother couldn't possibly understand. Susan was not aware of the whole situation, and Keera couldn't fully express everything she'd experienced. Instead, she just smiled up at her mother and told her that she would try. From that moment on, Keera did her best not to let her sadness show, hoping that her mother did not offer any more advice.

Thankfully, Keera didn't have to pretend for long because school came along again quickly. Once school began, Keera was excellent at masking her emotions. She no longer let small things bother her, or, at the very least, let it show that they bothered her. It seemed like the new and confident Keera attracted the attention of kids in her school, as well. All the girls wanted to be her friend, and all the boys wanted to be around her. She felt normal and, for whatever reason, her mind opened up and outsider's thoughts came to her easy. Keera liked the attention and was grateful to not be so lonely at school but deep inside, she still felt alone amidst the thoughts of the people around her. The feeling of being whole began to crack under the pressure, and a missing piece began to form; small at first, but the piece grew nightly, with each dreamless sleep without Grand Father. Each day also brought more noise and thoughts in her mind, which led to less sleep, and the need to pretend things were fine even more. Keera couldn't understand how she was now able to hear so much through her mind. All alone, she also didn't know how she was ever going to figure out how to stop it from happening.

She was beginning to feel resentment toward her mother, and the relationship her sisters had with each other. Things seemed easy for them and Keera felt trapped because she was unable to control what was happening to her, or tell her secrets to anyone who would understand. She no longer wanted friends. She just wanted the world to quiet down around her, and to be whole again. Every day ended on the same note. Keera would exit her school bus and begin walking toward her home with her head down, using the worn path to walk up to her house, and her intuition to sense when she was close enough to her waiting mother. Once she was close enough to Susan, she would take a deep breath, clear her mind, and put on the most normal after-school 'I had a great day' face she could muster. Susan accepted it every time.

One afternoon, after school was back in session for a few

months, Keera was at her wits' end with the people around her. She was done pretending that she was okay and that every day at school was a great day. She never struggled with schoolwork but the emotional turmoil she felt, inside and around her, was beginning to affect everything, and that was enough to make her want to burst. She decided she was going to go home and tell her mother everything. She would do what she needed to do, in order to prove to her mother that what she said was the truth. She knew that her mother would try and fix her, but things were so bad that maybe she did need to be fixed.

Before the bus came to a complete stop, Keera sensed a change in the energy. As the bus was approaching her house, there was a bright light shining right where her mother would be standing, waiting for her bus. It was as if the sun was shining from inside the house, peeking out through the front door. Someone was at her house, but the sun was so bright, she did not know who it was. The bus screeched to a halt and Keera rose from her seat, without taking her eyes off the light, she walked toward the front of the bus. She took a moment to stand at the exit and stare at the light. Although she could not see anyone in front of her house, she knew her mother was there. She could hear her mother's thoughts. They were about her and were full of excitement. No matter how hard she reached out, she could not hear the thoughts of whoever was with her mother. It was strange to feel a presence, but not hear anything. Keera stepped off the bus, squinting and more curious, than anything else.

Keera approached her front door, where she could hear

her mother and a man speaking in very professional tones. As she got closer to the house, it felt as if she stepped into a veil and was no longer blinded by the light, but enveloped by it.

"Oh, there she is! Keera, honey, come meet Mr. Iftiin." Keera walked cautiously toward her mother, who's waving a handful of papers wildly, and Mr. Iftiin, who is standing there looking not at her, but Keera felt he was looking through her. He had the most beautifully soul-piercing, brown eyes and smooth brown skin. He had black and grey hair that looked to be long and tied in a ponytail. She felt like she knew him, but couldn't place where she had seen him before. He was extremely tall, taller than anyone Keera had known.

Keera turned to her mom, "Hi, Mom." She then turned to their guest and gave a tentative smile. "Nice to meet you, Mr. Iftiin." He gave a big smile, then bent down to address Keera. He chuckled lightly, as if hearing her confused thoughts. "It's nice to *formally* meet you, Keera." Mr. Iftiin spoke in a low, yet powerful, deep voice. He spoke as if he and Keera were in on an inside joke. Keera almost caught a glimpse of a memory, but the moment slipped by. "Oh," Susan broke Keera's deep thought, and Mr. Iftiin's attention on Keera. Without missing a beat, Mr. Iftiin responded, "Ah yes, Susan, Keera may not remember me. As I told you, I am the very new guidance counselor. Recognition will take some time." Keera smiled and nodded, giving Susan the reassurance that she needed. Keera needed to find out who Mr. Iftiin really was, but she didn't want her mother to worry. She knew that he meant no harm, even if she didn't know who he was or what he was thinking. "Like I said, I am in charge of the gifted program, so you won't find me on the regular school roster. I am hired by the state and will counsel outside of school," Mr. Iftiin reiterated his points again, for Keera's benefit. "Consider me your daughter's after-school enrichment. My purpose is to help my students reach their full potential, so that they may conquer the world." Mr. Iftiin gave Keera a little smile, "But of course, it is up to the students if they want to participate."

Keera looked at Mr. Iftiin and smiled before looking at her mother. She felt excitement swelling within her, which told her that this would be beneficial. Susan saw real excitement across her daughter's face, for the first time in a long time. "Keera, I will let you decide." Keera thought for a moment. It bothered her that she couldn't remember where she had seen him before. I know him, she thought to herself. It just would not come to her. She already knew what she wanted to do, and why. Keera loved school and never said no to learning more. If Mr. Iftiin was going to be involved, she would figure out where she'd seen him before. "Mr. Iftiin, I accept." A look of relief flashed across Mr. Iftiin's face before returning to his calm and jovial expression. "Great! We will get started next week. Your mother and I will first take care of the paperwork, and then you and I will start the real work." Susan told Keera that she would walk Mr. Iftiin to his car to talk about the next steps and that she should go inside to start her homework. As Mr. Iftiin walked away, Keera could feel his energy leave with him. She turned to watch them walk away. Just as she turned, like a balloon, the veil popped and Mr. Iftiin became blocked by the sun again. Trying once more, Keera reached out, sending one telepathic message - *I know you.* Without missing a beat, she received a message back - *We'll meet again, young Keera.* Grand Father.

That day, The Grand Father walked into Keera's life. He made sure to integrate himself within her school and home, so that he could continue to train her. No longer did Keera feel afraid or alone. With Grand Father, she knew that she would continue learning and find peace.

PART II
WORLDS COLLIDE

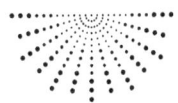

CHAPTER EIGHT

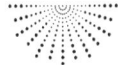

Here's to 18 years

<u>Keera</u>

*J*looked round the living room at Thena, preparing the house for my birthday gathering. It's just Thena, Mara, and me. It had been hard, since our mother was no longer around. Thena and Mara have been taking care of me since our mom disappeared. *Man, five years now.* It's still a mystery. There was no trace of her, so there was nothing the police could do to bring her back. I found myself thinking about her often, wishing she were still here, but my sisters and I have coped as best as we can and I know one day we will be reunited. *I miss her.*

"Where's the drink?" I slapped my forehead, forcing my face toward the ceiling. I had found a recipe from my father's cookbook for an alcohol-like drink he used to love when he was back home. I didn't have all the original ingredients, but he once told me that the substitutes found here would do the trick. It took me months to find all the ingredients, and I was going to enjoy this moment if it was the last thing I did. "How could you forget when it was all you talked about for six months, Keera!?" I looked back at Thena and gave her a sly smile.

My sisters had also baked my favorite treat from my father's cookbook for my birthday. It was supposed to be a surprise, but they should have known I would find out. It's hard to keep secrets from someone who, without trying, receives information from anyone who's near. I was taught very well by my father. He taught me to be respectful when trying to enter someone's mind, but because it was just about my birthday, I felt that it would be okay to gather information without permission. My sisters knew I would pick their brains and they tried to block me out. Thena had successfully hidden the secret in her mind, but Mara never could create a strong enough wall. Regardless, I hadn't told them that I had been practicing non-stop to improve my ability, especially since mom's disappearance. *Mom, I will find you.*

I made my way to the kitchen, grabbed the cookbook, and started preparing the recipe. Putting on my most innocent smile and busying myself with the recipe, I said, "Thena, I haven't totally forgotten. I've had *other* things on my mind." Thena looked at me and then gasped. "Sometimes you need to just forget you can do that, Keera. I mean, shit, how will we ever surprise you with anything?" She threw up her hands. "I give up. Just make sure you follow the rules and not to pry in our heads where it's super private." I rolled my eyes, "I know, I know. Trust me, there are things about you, I would rather not kn—."

A pillow hit my mouth, stopping the words short. I squinted my eyes, glaring at Thena, preparing my attack. We were at full war. Pillows were flying everywhere. Laughter filled the room and I felt myself relaxing a little. "Hey guys, I know you're having fun and all, but there is a lot to be done before people get here for the party. Or have y'all forgotten?" Mara walked in, tidying as she spoke. She was the nurturing, mothering type out of the three of us. She took the lead when mom disappeared and always made sure we had everything we needed. I loved her for that. Personally, I thought she needed to go out and date, get a boyfriend, or at least get laid but she never listens to my suggestions. She always says, 'When you grow up, you will understand.' Well, I'm 21, now, and I still don't understand why she is so hard on herself. Life is too short to keep letting any fun fall through the cracks.

I put on my biggest puppy dog impersonation. "Mara, it's my birthday!! Can't you let go and have fun for once? Pleeeaaasse???" I batted my eyes and slowly approached her, bringing my hands up in a prayer. From the corner of my eye, I saw Thena preparing to throw a pillow in Mara's direction. Because Mara was so focused on me, she did not have time to brace for the assault. Just as she was about to give in to me, the pillow hit her right square in her face. Her head bobbled and the time stopped. Thena and I braced for her reaction. I brought my hands up to my mouth to stifle my laughter. I was not sure how long we sat there staring, but it felt like an eternity. Mara rolled her eyes and growled as she picked up the pillow. She gave the pillow a few punches before throwing it back at Thena. The pillow made contact with Thena's chest. The shock registering on her face caused me to burst into laughter. Mara joined in and the pillow fight continued.

We all had a pillow in hand, hitting each other and screaming whenever a pillow hit its target. It all happened so fast. Mara's face dropped, causing alarm in Thena. Mara dropped the pillow she was holding, just in time for my pillow to make impact with her stomach. My laughter died when I noticed her expression. She held her hands up as if she was in a robbery. I looked around. There were a group of people, I think they were people, towering over us with laser-type guns pointed in our faces.

All joy and blood drained from my face. I couldn't understand what was going on. One minute I was having the best birthday of my life, the next I was afraid for my life. I was being yelled at in some language that was familiar, yet foreign to me. When I reached out to their minds, I couldn't even get into the surface. *Wow*. When I focused on the speaker, I could understand their language, but not enough to understand the situation. I tried translating, "….don't….up….check…." from a person, a guy, who was flinging his arms around. He left the circle and went to the coffee table, where my father's cookbook was lying on the floor, "…sense….belong to… Grand Father was here." Another person began to talk. I was trying to grasp what they were saying, but the only words I could understand were: Grand Father. I looked down, swallowed up in deep thought: *They were looking for my father*. He'd once told me that he was called grandfather among his people. I referred to him as my father because he was the only father figure in my life. My dad left us when I was very young and, since he was my mom's age, I couldn't very well call him grandfather.

I reached inside myself and conjured the pure joy I kept deep inside. In an instant, I understood what was going on and everything made sense. Once I knew what to do, I found my confidence. In their native tongue, I spoke, "Reh Tof-Narg se baogn!" I kept my eyes to the ground, afraid of what might happen next. There was a long silence so I slowly looked up. I was met with bewildered eyes, my sisters included. I looked around and the circle of eyes stared back at me in confusion. It was like a dream. I took a good look at them and their guns. I never thought I would be face-to-face with others like my father. He hid his true form from most people. My sisters didn't even know what he looked like. To them, my father was a man, six feet tall with tanned skin, a muscular build, jet-black long hair that was always tied in a low ponytail. He had hazel eyes that sparkled in the sun. His eyes were always the dead giveaway. They would change to a golden color and ripple like a pool when he showed any sign of emotion. But my mother and I knew what he was, and what he looked like. In the comfort of our home, when my sisters weren't around, he shed his façade and walked around proud. He was beautiful. It was as if his skin was alive. It was bronze with symbols tattooed, covering what I believed was his whole body. It was cosmic and unearthly beautiful. The symbols were also bronze and blended in with his skin tone. They were raised and appeared to dissolve and move around, subtly. Whenever I looked closely, the symbols were never in the same place as the last time. I remember asking him about it when he first came to us. He told me it was the cause of evolution:

'The symbols are actually the dead language of my planet. Each being is born with the history of our world written on their body. I guess because we neglected to keep records of our history, we have evolved in a way that it will never be forgotten… even if we cannot translate. I believe that one day our history will be translated and we will have order restored.'

I was amazed at his level of hope and since that moment, I wished that he was my true father. I asked why no one of his kind was able to touch another person and use their psychic ability to figure out the past. He told me that, because the words were ever-changing, it surpassed anyone's ability to focus long enough to get a clear reading. He was so wise and had lived so long. He appeared to be around my mom's age. but I knew that he had been around a lot longer than that.

I came back into the present and looked around. I could tell that the whole group was young. Although they had flight suits on, I saw the symbols on their exposed skin. If I didn't have a clue about the skin, I would not have even seen them moving. There were three males and one female. They all had similar features. I was unsure if they were related, or if the whole planet looked the same. But, like us humans, they ranged in sizes. The female was the smallest, but was not small by our standards. She was at least 5'10" and of medium build. I could tell that she was not one to mess with. She was beautiful. She had long blond hair that went down to her waist, a curvy, yet muscular, body and high cheekbones and beautiful grey almond-shaped eyes. The guy to the left of her had the same blond hair and grey eyes, almost menacing, but was at least five inches taller than her. He was bulky, if I didn't know any better, I'd say that he was juiced up. To his left, there was a guy who had bright red hair with streaks of purple. The purple almost looked like it glowed. His eyes were an incandescent purple. *Renegade*. I could tell that he was slightly older than the rest, but still younger than my father. He was about six feet tall and just as muscular as the rest. Finally, I looked at the one to the renegade's left, who looked the most like my father. He was about 6'2" with long black hair that flowed to the middle of his back. He had the same eyes as my father, and was slender, yet very muscular. I was lost in his eyes. He looked at me with wonder and I couldn't help but look away as my face heated. There was a pregnant pause before the tall, slender yet muscular, one spoke. He did not speak English but I understood some, "…them and watch… handle… one." He pointed at me with an intense stare. After a few seconds of staring, he said, in his native tongue, "You, up now!" He turned his hand over, gesturing to stand. Without another thought, I reached up and grabbed his hand. When our hands touched, electric sparks pulsed through my body. I'm not sure if he felt it, too, but by the way his irises rippled, I know he felt some type of emotion in that moment. When I was standing completely up, he let go of my hand and turned to walk out the door. I began to follow without even thinking. I wondered if he was somehow controlling me, and at the same time, I knew that he didn't have to because I was ready to follow him. I didn't even look back at my sisters for them to give me a reassuring smile that said, "Everything is going to be okay." I knew in my heart that I was going in the right direction.

Raknico

As I walk back to the ship, I can't help but wonder why the coordinates retrieved from the first ship were here, in this habitation. There aren't many people around for miles. It seems isolated, especially for our kind. We had reached our destination in record time. It may have taken us ninety Earth days to get here, but I am glad that I can finally start my mission to find The Grand Father and his team. The Grand Father is the leader of our race, but most importantly, he is my father. He left our planet eleven Earth years ago. The team made regular reports about their findings while here. Five Earth years ago, their reports said that they had accomplished their mission and were going to come home. I waited and waited for their arrival, yet none ever came, I knew something was not right. I was too young to rule at the time, and was not allowed to make executive decisions. Since I am the sole heir to the throne, I had to wait until I was of legal ruling age to avenge my father. During the time between my father's disappearance and my ruling, the High Appointed ruled and led our people. Instead of idly waiting, I trained and grew strong, in mind and body, to defeat my enemy.

In the corner of my eye, just slightly, I see her. I can't help but wonder about the female that is following close behind me. She is a very peculiar one, and she knows our native tongue. She also has psychic powers. I felt her attempting to enter my mind when we interrupted their fun fight, which was a very strange ritual. When we landed and came up to the dwelling, there was loud yelling and bouts of angry female voices. When we approached, it was to the sound of laughter and the three females wrestling on the floor seemed to be enjoying themselves. We all stopped and watched the exchange. It was very strange to us. I remember Shanluk asking me in my mind if we should just let them destroy each other and not get our hands dirty. The more I focused, the more I felt the love between the three. They were kindred. All three human females had black hair and smooth, caramel skin. It seemed that not a moment after that, the others in my group were coming to the same realization. I closed my eyes to absorb that positive energy. *So pure.* Not even a human minute goes by, when I hear lasers charging. I opened my eyes to see the group aiming their guns while one of the human females was raising a fluffy fabric sack above her head. She dropped the sack and kept her hands raised, as a sign of surrender. She was afraid. Shanluk left the group and bent down to collect something. It was my father's book of spells. Shanluk continued to raise his voice at the human females when Saniyah approached him and tried to talk him down. I loved my kin, Saniyah. She is a skilled empath and whenever Shanluk is around, we needed her to bring his energy back up. We seemed to get back on track when the human female with the shortest black hair spoke. She shocked us all; even her kin. We all stared at her. She told us, in my native tongue, that my father was here. It was obvious that he was no longer here, and hadn't been for some time. I could barely sense his energy. I immediately wanted to know more. She looked up and I was captivated by her brown eyes. They were the most beautiful eyes I've ever seen. The only other eyes that were comparably as beautiful belonged to my mother. That is all I remember of my mother. I was young when she ceased to exist. I have dreams of her, which I think are actual memories, where she is staring at me in my bed, saying goodbye. I reach for her, but she turns and creeps away. The dream usually ends there, with me waking up in a sweat wondering what happened. My father refused to talk about her. He told me that she ceased to exist and I should hold on to my happy memories and not dwell on the loss. My father is wise, and he always has my well-being at heart. So I always used my happy memories to block out the sadness I felt after my dreams. Looking into this human's eyes brought a bit of sadness to me. I pulled away from it and thought about the days when my mother held me in her arms tight as I drifted off to sleep. I could look past the similar beautiful eyes, but I could not seem to look past her beauty. She was like none I have ever seen. Her face was perfection, but her energy was the purest I have ever felt. She energized me like I was at home. The positive energy of the people and animals create a euphoric environment. No amount of work tires me, and I rarely sleep. I didn't think I would find that anywhere else. But here, in this isolated place, I feel at home.

She had information that I wanted, and needed, to know. As the leader of my group, I felt it was necessary that I be the one to interrogate her. I also couldn't help being pulled toward her. I didn't want anyone near her so, instead of making a fool of myself as I was plagued by emotional weakness, I took the leadership approach. When I tried to use my mind to force her to follow me, I was shocked when she didn't immediately obey. I have never been in a position where I could not use my mind to coerce someone inferior. It was a skill that all Grand Fathers have by birthright, yet she resisted. I needed to know how.

Since I had yet to absorb their human language, I could not

fully communicate. I singled her out by pointing and held out my hand to signal. She understood. She grasped my hand while rising. I was shocked, and then further shocked, when I felt a surge in energy. I had never felt anything like that and I didn't understand why, but she has to be important, somehow. I took a moment to meditate and ingest this culture. It is imperative that I learn their language so that we may communicate. She doesn't seem like she could hold my father prisoner, but I have to keep my guard up... especially since she did not obey my orders or mind persuasion.

CHAPTER NINE

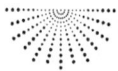

Keera

I didn't expect to be treated like royalty, but I expected to be treated better than this, especially since I can speak their native language. They treat me like a criminal. Do they think I put a gun to my father's head and forced him to teach me his language? That is absolutely insane! Terafey, my father, gave me many things and one was the gift of his native language. I just wish I had paid more attention to his lessons, because if I had, I would be able to communicate better.

I gladly follow the tall, slender, muscular one; the one with my father's eyes. From the moment I felt the spark, I've wanted to be close to him. I want to know more about him, like how he was related to my father. I don't even know his name. For now, I think I will call him, *Mr. Gorgeous.* He is so hot, and has such a serene face, it makes me feel at ease whenever I look at him.

I jump at the sound of a door sliding shut and locking. I turn to see that I am locked in, alone. He led me to the ship and I followed him right into my holding cell. *Stupid, stupid!* It looks like a hotel suite, but I know better. It is more like jail, and I'm not sure how long my sentence will be. The room is a nice size. From my viewpoint in front of the door, I see the room in its entirety. To my right, there is a desk and chair, with a mirror on the wall above it. Nothing but a pad of paper and a vase full of flowers are on it, and no doubt they are using the mirror to spy on me. Directly in front of me is a bed with lavish bedding. It looks nice and fluffy, but I will not allow myself to enjoy it. There are nightstands with lamps on them to the left and right of the bed. There are twin windows above the nightstands. It is a relief that I will be able to look outside, and at least get a taste of freedom. Then, finally, on my left there is a door that leads to a bathroom, I presume. I turn around and try the knob. I know that it will be locked, but I have to try it anyway. I bang on the door with my fists. Then I think of my sisters. They have to be terrified. I, at least, know a little about what I'm dealing with, but they have no clue.

When the group, led by Terafey, came, both of my sisters were away with their dad. They called many times and only came home once or twice that year. They just thought Terafey was our mom's new boy toy, which meant he wasn't staying long enough for them to care to get to know him. I, on the other hand, was fascinated by him. His voice lulled me. He reminded me of when I was a child in need of a protector. He gave me strength and hope, when all was lost. I remember the day he came for our first guidance session, I was outside playing with my dolls. My mom had told me that it was about time I gave up dolls, but I just couldn't give them up. They were my friends. Now that I look back on it, the dolls were probably the reason I didn't have any real friends. Anyway, there I was on my porch, playing with my dolls. I was telling my doll Suzy that it was time to get ready for the party when all of a sudden, it felt like the sun disappeared. I looked up to see what was blocking my light, and there he was: Terafey. I knew him as Mr. Iftiin. He just plopped down on the porch with me, picked up my doll Daisy, and pretended to help Suzy get ready. We sat out there for maybe forty minutes before my mom noticed he was out there. Sometimes I think he hid himself from her so that we could talk and play, but he'd never tell me if it was so. We got Suzy ready and then he began to pretend to be Sammy, Suzy's date. He was a perfect Sammy. It was like he knew how I imagined Sammy to be and played him perfectly. We got to the party and Sammy asked Suzy to dance. We moved them to the pretend dance floor. As we danced, I noticed that Sammy was standing alone, with no help. I looked up at him, astonished, and he simply said, "You can do it, too!" I put the biggest smile on my face and said, "I can? Will you show me, Mister Iftiin?"

"Call me Fey, little Keera," he said coolly.

"Well, can you show me, Fey?"

"Of course I can. You are the reason I am here." I looked at him wide-eyed. He made me feel important. "Just think about Suzy standing up. When you have the thought in your mind, push it to her." I did what he told me to do, and Suzy shook. It reminded me of the times when I was too lazy to get up and get the remote for the TV. I would will the remote to come to me and it would shake a little and remain across the room until I stood up to retrieve it. I never thought anything of it, but there it was, happening again. Fey encouraged me to try it again and when I did, Suzy stood up. Both Suzy and Sammy started moving to the music in my head. Before I could truly enjoy the moment, my mother came out of the house and the dolls dropped. I knew in that moment that I couldn't let him go, but I didn't have to worry too much because he charmed my mother, as well.

I walk across the room and lay in the bed that was provided for me. It wasn't the worst, but I had to tell myself not to get too comfortable. Staring up at the ceiling, I began to drift into asleep.

I am startled awake. I'm not sure what startled me, but I open my eyes, calling my dream forward in an attempt to get more details. It was that same dream again. Every now and again, I have this dream where I am walking on clouds and there are crowds and crowds of people cheering. There is a man next to me, but I can't see his face. I always wake up frustrated because curiosity gets me every time. I just want to know who he is and, even more frustrating is the question that nags me in the deepest parts of my brain: Why is his identity a secret? As I lay here and try to see his face, I can almost make out his features. My dream, and his face, slip through my fingers as I realize the door is being unlocked. I snap into a seated position and try to finger-comb my hair, to look somewhat presentable, in case the person on the other side is *Mr. Gorgeous.* Just thinking about him makes me feel relaxed and excited, at the same time. I sit staring at the door, willing my heart to calm. The seconds tick by and I start to wonder why no one is entering. I do not trust myself to move forward. I am afraid that if whoever is on the other side of the door sees what I am doing as an escape attempt, I will not survive the night. I sit on the bed, with my knees to my chest, for what seems like an eternity. The door finally slides open and *He* walks in. *Mr Gorgeous* stood in the doorway with his arms folded across his chest and his eyes on me, unmoving and piercing. He looks just as calming as the first time our hands met. I find myself letting go of my knees and sliding my legs down until my toes touch the floor. For some reason, I feel that he is not going to be hostile toward me. I want answers and I am sure that he has some questions to ask, as well. Since he is not speaking up, I thought it was best that we get on with it. "Please, where is my family?" I spoke in his native tongue, which seems to be coming back to me like five years hasn't passed since I last spoke it. Life finally sparked in his eyes. "So it is true. You can speak my language?" Oh my goodness! *Mr. Gorgeous* just spoke English. His voice is like butter; smooth and deep, and it sped up my heartbeat again. "Oh, so now you can speak English?" I said, straightening my back and puffing out my chest. I focused on the remnants of my anger, trying to calm my breathing. I can't believe he is speaking English like he's known it all his life. "I just learned. How is it that you have come to know my native language? How do you know the Grand Father?" he spoke with urgency. I stand up and walk right into his personal space. He seems a little uneasy with this type of intimacy, but I don't care. I need him to know that I am not going to be taken advantage of, or mistreated. "How about a truth for a truth? You tell me some-thing and I reciprocate. Sound fair?" He takes a step back, pondering my proposal. After a brief moment, he nods. I turn and walk toward the mirror, "Are we being watched? Are there cameras here, invading my privacy?" I turn around, sharply, to face him. "No, we do not have such uses for recording devices," he said matter-of-factly. "My turn. How is it that you have come to know my native language?"

Without thinking too hard I respond: "Terafey taught me. He –"

"The Grand Father taught you our native language? For what purpose?"

"Why don't you have a use for *recording devices,* as you say?"

"We can view each others' memories, including inanimate objects." Raising his voice slightly, "Answer the question!" So they are clairvoyant and telekinetic, interesting. The room began to cool down. It felt like the energy was stirring and buzzing around us. "Oh yeah, I remember father saying som —" He stepped closer to me and yelled, "Father!? What is the meaning of this? The Grand Father has but one child." Raising my voice in return, I took a step closer to him, "I know he has a son back home but he was the only father figure I knew!" The energy in the room warmed up a bit. I lowered my voice, feeling hurt, "Father told me many stories about his brave and noble son. He said he will make a great leader someday. I just wanted a father like that." I took a few steps back. "He told me that on his planet he was called Grand Father. He looked my mom's age. I couldn't call him Grandfather. Here, a grandfather is an old grumpy guy with whiskers. Terafey was so not like that." I looked at Mr. Gorgeous. "He was beautiful. He was also a loving father. I remember many stories he told me of his son." This seems to interest him. *Mr Gorgeous* let the tension leave his body, causing a shift in the room. "What did he say about him?" I turn to the desk, pull out the chair, and sit down. I take a deep breath. "Well, I remember this one story in particular. He told me of a time when he took his son to watch him train the soldiers. They weren't physically training, it was all mental training. Well, the young boy did not want to be left out, so he asked his father if he could join in. Terafey, uh... Grand Father, didn't see any harm so he allowed him to join the ranks. They were practicing the art of manipulating inanimate objects. Well, his son was having difficulties, as he should. He got more and more frustrated. So much so that the energy was being affected. Terafey was about to go over and calm him down when the object blew up." I snap my fingers, trying to recall what the object was. *Damn it.* Mr. Gorgeous interrupted my thought, "What is the cause of your pause?" I smile. "I am trying to remember the name Father used for the object... I think it was a fruit. Oh yeah, it was --"

"Ahelpa!" We speak at the same time. I look up at him and find him smiling, as if reminiscing on a memory. Without thinking, I get up from the chair and walk toward him. I can feel the pull toward him. Without even touching, I feel the electricity flowing through my body. I am face to face with him. I open my mouth to speak and then close it. Before I can attempt to speak again, he turns and walks out the door. He turns, slightly, to look back," Your family is safe." He quickly turns away, shuts the door, and locks it. It is then when I know he is Raknico, Terafey's son. I place my forehead on the door, breathing deeply, while trying to absorb the information. I am in the presence of royalty again. *Lucky me.*

Raknico

As I stand outside her chambers, I can not erase the fact that she knew my father, was taught our language and, surprisingly, knows me as well. My father told her stories of me! He would only do that with someone he felt close to. Why didn't my father ever tell me about her? I need to know more, but after the exchange we just had, I am not sure I should get any closer. Before I even opened her door, I knew it was her behind it. It was like I felt her heart beating with mine. Something was drawing me closer and closer to her, and I did not ever want it to stop. I opened the door, but didn't trust myself to go any closer. Even being a few feet away was too close. I couldn't stop staring. She broke my trance when she spoke in my native language. This time it was smoother and almost native. My father worked with her vigorously; if only I knew the reason. *Keera.* Even her name brought comfort to me. My team and I studied her home and her sisters' memories. Thena and Mara did not reveal much about the Grand Father's time here. It seems they were away while Grand Father was doing his research. They thought my father was their mother's boyfriend and stayed away, so as not to get wrapped up in drama. I thought it was a laughable concept but, nonetheless, it was intel. Keera, sweet Keera. I need to get into her head but for some reason, I am blocked out. She seems to have all the details I need, and I cannot reach out and take them. Throughout our whole exchange I kept getting surged with energy. I even released large amounts of negative energy, but it seemed to do nothing to me or her but change the temperature in the room. Actually, it was amazing! It was like she could absorb the negative energy in the room, without being adversely affected. If our people could do that, we would not fear extinction or the Beneath. I place my hand on her door, receiving an electric shock. There is a reason why my father spent his time here. If he believed that she was important to the survival of our people, I am going to find out why.

Keera

I can feel him standing outside of my door. I did not see any movement or shadows but I know he is there. The moment he left, I felt emptiness. I can't explain it, but I know that I want him to be near. I can not fight the feeling. I am bored just standing by the door waiting for his return, so I walk back to the chair, sit down, and begin to twirl around in circles, thinking about Raknico. After about seven rotations, the energy in the room changes. I stop twirling and look up to see the Renagade. "So, Keera, it seems we have a few things to discuss," his deep voice rolled through the air. It seems like they all learned English and were now experts. The energy in the room stirred and the room began to chill. "I have nothing to say to you. Where are my sisters?"

Silence.

We do a stare-off. I can feel his anger growing. It isn't affecting me, but it is as if the anger is flying right to me. "Tell me what you know about Grand Father. Why was he with you, and for how long? Why are you being so difficult?" I am not being difficult! I'm not even sure how he arrived at that conclusion. I had had it at that point and my anger began to surface. How dare he come at me like this? I have been nothing but helpful. It is not my fault I was locked up and not given an opportunity to talk to anyone. "I am not being difficult. What I am being, is held against my will. I will tell you what you want to hear when I see my sisters. You can send that other guy back in here. I like him better."

I turn around and fold my arms across my chest. I can hear him breathing heavily behind me. I am angry and I increasingly became more and more agitated. After about five minutes, the door slid open, then closed and locked. The energy in the room went back to its normal state. I, on the other hand, did not feel so good.

Raknico

I sit, patiently waiting for Shanluk to return from interrogating Keera. I was nervous about sending someone into Keera's chamber. It wasn't just my nerves. I also did not want anyone near her. I feel like she is mine, like she was made for me. But at the same time, I needed someone to go in and see if they yielded the same results that I did when I was around her. I chose Shanluk. He is the perfect person because he is skilled at breaking mental walls and his energy has a larger range than most of us. He is the only person I know who can be consumed with so much negative energy, and not be absorbed into the Beneath.

I heard a loud noise outside my door. I can feel that it is someone very weak and near extinction. I quickly go to see who is out there; Shanluk. He is leaning against the wall, close to the floor. I reach out to him with my mind: *What happened?*

I don't know. I got upset and my negative energy was pulled from me. I am left with the little positive energy I had. This is an interesting revelation. Keera can absorb negative energy and is not weak from it. We have not seen this with any other human, or any other being for that matter. I reach out and project my positive energy to replenish Shanluk. He relaxes in my arms. I know he is resting and allowing the energy to take root in his cells. I teleport Shanluk to his chamber so that he can rest comfortably. I have to know more about Keera. Since she can take away energy from my crew, I think it is best that all communication go through me. I smile knowing that, in my heart, I would not have it any other way.

Keera

I can't sleep. I know it is well into the wee hours of the night. I am just so agitated and wound up. What is with all of this energy? After the renegade left, I have to run in place to burn off some energy. It is so weird. I walk from wall to wall in my room and am still too energized. I begin running in place again. I alternate between running in place, running from wall to wall, and running in circles. I stop to do a couple of reps of jumping jacks. The room begins to electrify. "Is this how you humans use your energy?" I blow out an exaggerated breath and turn to face Raknico. He looks at me smugly. "Really!? You think I'm here for your entertainment? I haven't been able to sit still since your little renegade friend left. What is up with him?" Raknico look at her, confused., "I don't understand? I am not entertained, simply curious." I take an exasperated breath. "Whatever. I would just like to go to sleep and dream a dream. Why are you here anyway, RaaaKnico?" I draw out his name to try to taunt him. I want him to feel pressure; to understand that I know things and that is why I am more valuable alive. "Hmm... I see you have connected the dots, Kee-ra," he looks at me with his eyebrow raised, "I am here to find out how you have the ability to absorb energy. How is it that you almost took all of Shanluk's essence?" I ponder that for a moment. I almost killed his friend. I had an abundant amount of energy that I somehow absorbed from the Renegade. Did I take it, or was it given to me? "So his name is Shanluk? Cute. I'm sorry, but I don't have any answers for you," I say as I begin running in place. "There has to be some way to turn it off, or send the energy back into the universe. We do not have this issue on—" I hold up my hand for him to stop speaking. It is rude but I don't want to lose the passing thought. As he spoke, a memory of my father and I talking came to mind. It was hazy and all I remember is him saying, "You can absorb it or deflect it. You need to understand both. It may save your life one day." I can't remember why we were having that conversation, but it seemed to have made sense to me now.

I close my eyes and shake my head to try to get back into the conversation. "I'm sorry, what were you saying?" I'm not looking at him, but I can feel his amusement. "Tell me, would you like me to help you burn off some of that energy?" I look up, narrowing my eyes, and shoot him a sharp look. He has a silly half-smile on his face. I think he has dimples. Mr. Gorgeous has sexy dimples? The thought increased my heart rate. His facial expression is almost creepy, but at the same time, it is filled with sexual promise. *I think?* I weigh my options. Stay up all night jumping around, or give in to

Raknico? I didn't realize that I was still bouncing around and constantly moving. My curiosity won. "What will you do and what do I have to do in return?" Raknico gave me a full smile and now I'm sure his beautiful face has dimples. "I won't hurt you, I promise, and all you have you do for me is continue to be honest and answer my questions. Do we have a deal?" I wasn't sure what he was going to do, but I knew he wasn't going to kill me and that was all I cared about at the moment. I nod. I am afraid of what is to come but also excited at the possibilities.

Raknico took a step closer to me. He leaned down to my ear and whispered, "Please relax, this will only take a second." I raise an eyebrow, "A second?" I laugh. The list of possibilities shortened as he put his hands over my shoulders. I feel an electric charge flow down my arms. He breathes in deep and the room begins to buzz. Little by little, the extra energy begins to flow from my body and out through his hands. He makes a few sounds like he is in pain, or maybe it is pleasure, but continues to draw out the extra energy until I feel calm enough to sleep. Once he is finished, he keeps his hands above my shoulders. I open my eyes and look up at his face. His eyes are still closed. I study his face. He looks like he is trying to compose himself and failing miserably. He finally opens his eyes and looks at me like he wants something that only I could provide. Without even thinking, I step up on my toes and plant my lips right on his. His eyes widen and then he pushes me away from him. He bows and says, "Good night, Keera," before walking out of the room. I whisper, "Thank you, good night," knowing he can not hear me. There is no way he did not feel the electric shock from our kiss. Our whole exchange was very informative. I now have to figure out how to deflect energy so that I don't mistakenly kill anyone. Now that I know I can absorb energy, I do not want to accidentally harm my family. Wait, would I harm my family, or just otherworldlies? This is getting more and more complicated. Suddenly, I feel a level of exhaustion I've never felt before, so I head to bed for the sleep I crave.

Raknico

I head straight for my chamber. I do not want to run into anyone from my crew. They would sense my extra energy and wonder how it is that Shanluk was almost drained dry, and I added extra time to my life force. It feels amazing. Keera is amazing! To think that she has the power to absorb negative energy and then turn it into something our people can use. I can now understand why my father did not speak about her. If anyone on the downward-slope toward the Beneath was to find out about her, they would surely try to abuse her abilities. Or worse, whoever is trying to destroy the Isle would try to destroy Keera, as well. I need to keep her safe. It is what my father would want, I'm sure of it. He has always told me, "Know your enemy through and through because you must believe that they know all about you." I must believe that my enemy is keeping me close and is following my every move. If I told anyone of Keera and her ability, she may not survive long enough to help me find Grand Father. *Oh Father, where are you?* I could really use some guidance right now.

CHAPTER TEN

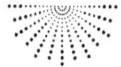

Two months later…

Keera

Staring at the ceiling, I can see the sun coming up from the horizon. I think we are still on Earth, but I can't be sure because I have never been on a spaceship. I wouldn't know if they navigated the skies like airplanes, or flew so smoothly that a person with the worst case of motion sickness would not get sick. At any rate, I have no motivation for the day so I don't even make a move to get up from the bed. The windows turned out to be more of a curse than a blessing. I have been confined to this room for what I believe is months, and I don't even see an end. As I lie here, I make a quick plan to cover the windows sometime today. I feel so depressed, and have so many thoughts and questions running through my head. *Where are my sisters? Are they still alive? Were they probed, like they do in the movies?* Each day seems to blend in with the next. I am brought breakfast and then given an hour to eat. A few hours later, they bring in lunch and a few hours after that, they bring me dinner. I tried to entertain myself with a game of trying to guess who will bring my meals, but they either read my weakened mind and change at the last moment, or there is no rhyme or reason to what they do. They try to provide us with food that we are accustomed to, but for some reason, after eating their version of food for months, the food just makes me sick. I nibble on anything they give me, just to try to calm my stomach. They have given me a few books and outdated magazines to read, but nothing of interest. I woke one day to a couple pictures from my house lying beside me on the bed. I'm sure it was a nice gesture from Raknico, to help me feel at home, but all it did was make me more depressed. I've asked for a television, but their ship does not have electrical outlets. Why the freck don't they have electricity where they come from? I don't even have the will to bathe or eat. I do manage to bathe on the days Raknico comes in to question me. After our kiss, I think two months ago, things got a little more interesting. I think that we began to trust each other and, with that, we shared information. There is something about him that I just can't put my finger on, but I like it.

The door opens. Someone walks in to set my breakfast down and walks out, without speaking. The whole crew, with the exception of Raknico, never speaks to me. I think they are afraid that I may inadvertently suck all of their energy. I mean, seriously, it was an accident! Raknico told me that he told his crew it was not me that almost drained Shanluk. He told them that Shanluk must have interacted with some human thing that they have never come across. It worked out, because Shanluk didn't have much memory from our visit, but Raknico added that I had to promise never to do it again. So far, I have kept my promise but deep inside, I think the crew still fears me, despite anything Raknico has said. I don't really care. I don't want to interact with any of them besides Raknico. Since day one, he has done something to me. Even now, he tries to ignore the sparks and avoid touching me. He believes there is nothing special in our reaction to each other. Every couple of days, when he comes by, I say, "You don't feel that?" He always responds with, "Nothing unusual," then he continues with his questioning. It's only a matter of time before the truth is revealed. What's that saying? It will all come out in the wash? I guess I will wait. Until then, I will play the game the way he wants to play.

Raknico

We've been here for a couple of Earth months and still there are no leads toward the whereabouts of The Grand Father and his crew. We keep the sisters because they were the last to interact with the missing crew. I am beginning to feel like they just vanished, but cannot figure out what happened to the ship. I've been questioning Keera every other day, to see if I can draw out any new details that differ from what she has told me in past interrogations. She has many stories of her time with the Grand Father. She has had some great times with my father, and I am envious of that time they have shared.

Of all the stories that I've heard, the story that is most vital to me is the day his ship left Earth. This day is significant to her, as well, because it is also the day her mother disappeared. I find that fact peculiar, because from what I understand, my father and her mother cared for each other. I feel there is deception all around that day, but I cannot confirm without being able to see her memories from that day, or find someone from my father's crew. I feel pain for Keera every time I ask her to tell me about that day. The first time she spoke of her mother's disappearance, I did all that I could not to run to her and comfort her. She is getting better about hiding her emotions about that day. I know she still feels depressed about it, so I reach out to her mentally so that she doesn't hurt as much. I don't relieve all the pain, because I don't want her to know that I sympathize with her. She knows that I lost my mother when I was really young, but does not point out the fact to make me feel bad. No matter the emotions she expresses while telling the story, the fact remains that each time she tells the story, there is no detail different from the very first time she recounted it to me.

I have reached an end. I do not know if I can continue to hold these humans against their will. Not just for their health, but for the health of my crew. Their human sadness is affecting my crew and I need to fix that problem before anyone gets any weaker. Everyone thinks that there is something going on that I have not told them. When Shanluk almost expired, it was luck that he did not remember the events of that night. I was able to get the heat off of Keera and blame his weakness on an unexplained Earthly rarity, that would hopefully never happen again. Although they won't speak up, I know that they are still fearful of being in the room alone with Keera. Besides the facts around the Shanluk incident, there is nothing more for me to divulge. They are all getting weaker and I am staying strong. I tell them that I am keeping my thoughts and feelings positive, because I cannot tell them about absorbing energy from Keera.

She tells me that she feels a spark when we touch. I feel the same spark, but I cannot explain why, so I simple deny it. The crew confronted me about this. I was sitting at my desk, facing the wall, when they came into my chamber. They were all very angry about the condition of the humans. It was Saniyah who approached me first, "Knico, we need to talk. How is it that we have not remedied this drain? Why not bring the sisters together, so that we may benefit from their gathering?" I looked at the plea in her eyes. Then I looked at Shanluk. "Please Nic, what else can we do? I'm trying to survive this mission." Although Shanluk had changed since that incident with Keera, he was the same self-preserving male I knew. I thought it was a good idea, but I wasn't sure if we should because, although Keera's mind is weakening, she still may be able to escape with her sisters and leave us in a worse position. They were our only hope to piecing together the disappearance of our people, and I did not want to harm our chances. The whole crew looked to me for a response. I took a deep breath before responding, "I know that is the right thing to do but we should not meditate on their energy before we get our own emotions and energy in order. Try—" Before I could finish, Shanluk interjected, "We've tried! It's very diffi-cult when the only available energy is negative and sad," he paused. "And so dark," he continued in an ominous voice. Everyone in the room shifted and became uneasy. I knew of the dark energy he was referring to. It was so difficult not to feel it, especially when it was in the same room as you. I felt like everyone was being reasonable, except Kemorte, my kin. Kemorte's presence now sends chills down my spine. His life-force is turning grey. I have seen this many times, right before someone falls from grace. I do not know what will become of him if he does fall so far from home. Just as I finished reflecting on the darkness, Kemorte spoke up, "Look, we've questioned them and questioned them. There's nothing new to be said and, quite frankly, I'm exhausted. Who cares if something happens to them while we energize our beings? I mean, I know you care, since you are almost as pure as a newborn. Tell me, Raknico, how do they make you so pure? Do they do some human act that pleasures you, so that you release all negative energy? Having three sisters at your disposal must make you feel powerful! And that Keera, she's a firecracker. Is that why you keep her all to yourself?" I sat quietly, but Kemorte was not pleased with my silence, "ANSWER ME!" I didn't want to be confronted with this, but I knew for the sake of the rest of the crew, I couldn't just let it linger. My anger was already rising high because he was speaking so ill about Keera, but I could not let any of them know that I cared. Kemorte yelled toward me again, "ANSWER ME, RAKNICO!" I shot back, "I DON'T KNOW WHY I'M MORE PURE!" It was the truth. I did not know why the energy available from Keera was more pure than any energy I had experienced while here on Earth, and possibly ever in my existence. Lowering my voice, I continued, "I feel the same stress on my being as all of you. I am not doing anything different when I interact with them. I cannot help the fact that for some reason you all are afraid to be in the same room as Keera for longer than a minute. I even try to give some of my energy, and you all refuse. What else can I do?" Without giving anyone a chance to speak, I continued, "Fine. Let's let them gather and see how that changes things. The first moment any one of them shows signs of distress, or if anyone runs, we are separating them and looking for other solutions." I stood up and walked out of my own chamber, leaving them to watch my departure. There was somewhere I needed to be anyway.

Keera

The day flies right by and before I know it, I have to shower and get ready for my interrogation with Raknico. Right on schedule, Raknico walks into my room for another game of 'Will the story change?' I don't know how many times he expects me to tell him what I know about my Father and what he did while he was here. I especially hate when he asks me to tell him the story about the day they left. Not only did I lose the only father I knew, I also lost my mother. It still haunts me that she just disappeared with no note or trace. How come the police can't locate her, or at least locate a body, to give me closure? It's been years and I still can't let it go. Even after telling the story a million times, I still get emotional. Raknico will never tell me, but I know he uses his empathic psychic abilities to take away some of the pain of those memories. He only takes away the painful surface, just enough where I do notice his help.

He walks in the room and I give him the strongest smile I

can muster up. "Good evening, Raknico. What questions do you have for me today?" I approach him and he nervously steps back. "Good evening, Keera. I am not staying. There will not be any questions tonight." I give him a confused look, "Huh? What's going on? Are you going to finally let us go? Speaking of which: how are my sisters? Are they ok? I miss them so much." Tears start to form in my eyes. I don't care that he will see me cry, I am so past the point of a break down. "Please don't lose hope. I've come to tell you that you will be allowed time with your sisters." I can't hold in my excitement, "REALLY!? Oh my goodness, why the change?" As he walks back to the door he responds, "Well, the sadness you and your sisters are feeling is negatively affecting our life forces. I don't know about you humans, but we are all out of sync because of the stress." I think for a second, "You know, you're right. I do feel a little…" Before I could finish my sentence, he was gone.

CHAPTER ELEVEN

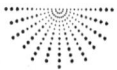

Keera

*I*t was three days before I was finally allowed to see my sisters. I couldn't believe that Raknico had told me that I would be allowed to see my sisters, but didn't tell me when. He was lucky that he was not the one to escort me to the "gathering hall." The next time I saw him, I would have a few choice words about schedules, how they should make some, and what it means to effectively communicate.

I started my day like I always do: staring at the ceiling, cursing those damn windows. Every day I make a plan to cover them, and by the end of the day I tell myself that if I cover the windows, I am accepting this as my fate. I expected someone to come in, bring my breakfast, and leave. For the first time since my birthday, someone other than Raknico spoke to me. It was the female; I believe her name was Saniyah. It's a weird name, Sa-Ny-yah, it sounds almost exotic. "Good morrow, Keera. I am here to escort you to the gathering hall to be with your kin." I thought she spoke very old English-like, but I liked it. "Awesome! I wasn't expecting this today, since I wasn't informed. Do you think I can have a minute to freshen up?" She nodded and then exited.

I hurried to the bathroom to brush my teeth, wash my face, and brush my hair. It had grown since we've been here and they refuse to give me a pair of scissors to cut it. It didn't matter because I was finally seeing my sisters today. They wouldn't care if my hair started sprouting flower buds. Saniyah must have thought I meant literally a minute because as I walked out of the bathroom, she was already in the room, waiting patiently. She was facing the desk and was holding something in her hand. As I walked out of the bathroom, her back tensed a little, "You use recording devices to record events." It wasn't a question. "How do you record the emotion behind the events, if you do not use your mind? Holding this photograph in my hand, I can see the event but I can't *feel* the emotion. You look like you were all happy." It felt good being able to talk to someone other than Raknico, "Well, we're not completely inept. We remember the emotion with our mind. It's like the picture serves as a visual reminder to our brain. Like a memory card for a computer..." I trailed off, remembering that they don't have computers, "Well, let's just say our minds need a little help sometimes. With pictures, we bring the memory to the forefront of our minds and our brain automatically recalls the emotion of the event." Saniyah didn't respond. She just put the picture down and walked toward the door, motioning for me to follow her. This was the first time I actually paid attention to the ship. The walls pulsed and hummed. It was beautiful. I reached out to touch it and it warmed my skin. I tried not to follow too closely to Saniyah. Although she spoke to me, I could still feel the tension roll off of her, so I kept a safe distance.

We reached a set of doors where she put her hand up to a pad on the wall, then the hatch on the door unlocked. The doors split open and, by peeking past Saniyah, I could see one of my sisters. I rushed past yelling, "Thank you, Saniyah!" I ran right into Mara's embrace. "Oh my God! I thought I lost you. Are you okay? Did they do anything to you?" I held her so tight, like my life depended on it. "Mara, I'm fine. I am better now. How are you? Where is Thena?" On cue, Thena walked in after being escorted by Shanluk, "I'm right here, silly nut!" Thena rushed into our embrace and we sat there and cried. It was the happiest day I thought I'd never see.

Raknico

There was a shift in the energy and I realized that all three human females were, once again, united. So far, allowing the sisters to see each other was going well. I could feel everyone around me start to strengthen. There were smiles that I haven't seen in a long time. Everyone was smiling, except for Kemorte. His energy lightened up a little, but I could still feel that he was on edge about something. I had to know so I reached out mentally: *What's wrong Kem, does this not please you?* Kemorte just looked at me with a devious grin, then got up and walked out of the room. Before he cleared the doorway, he finally responded telepathically, *Oh, I will be pleased when this is all over.* The way he spoke felt like there was more meaning to his words. I didn't know what that meant, but I knew something was not right with him. I reached out to Saniyah's mind, *Something is not right with your brother.* She gave me a look, then spoke with her eyes, *I know, I have been feeling it for some time.* I tap my finger to my chin. *Watch him and report anything unusual.* Saniyah nodded. I am glad that bringing the sisters together was going well. I had a feeling that the team would need to be at their strongest, going forward.

Keera

Thena, Mara, and I finally finished crying. We spoke about what was going on the last few months, just catching up on our boredom. While we were crying, someone brought us food and drinks. We all grabbed plates and, for the first time in weeks, the food was not all bad. It was like normal Earth food!

When Mara got up to be escorted to the bathroom, I used that time to talk to Thena privately. I would have spoke to them both, but Mara is too much of a mom to hear what I was about to tell Thena. "So tell me, for real, how have you been Keera? Has Raknico been okay? Every time I mentioned your name, I swear he would blush. I think he likes you. He is kinda cute!" Thena took the time to tease me about Raknico. I didn't mind, because I felt the same way. "I'm fine. I, um, actually have to tell you something." She looked at me like I was about to tell her I have cancer. I took a deep breath, "Raknico and I... well, we sort of got a thing going on. Or, HAD a thing going on... before he demanded that I suppress his memories of us so that the others wouldn't find out." I spit it all out so fast that

I had to inhale more air. Thena's jaw dropped and she started stammering, trying to find the right words to say. A smile slowly crept onto her face, "Da…yu..mmm..You mean, you were flirting with the enemy? You dog, you!" She laughed out loud briefly before I shushed her with my hand over her mouth. I didn't want Mara to hear anything because she would demand that I tell her everything and I have a hard time lying to her. Thena, on the other hand, lied like it was her business. I had to get it all out so she could give me advice before Mara returned. She stopped laughing, "Wait. How did you suppress his memories? Where'd you learn to… have you ever done that to us?" I ignored her questions and continued, so that I could get it all out, "That's not all." She looked at me patiently so I continued, "We went all the way." I waited for Thena to say something. I would have settled for a look, but her face went blank and she was mute. I shook her violently, "Thena, say something!" It seemed to do the trick. "What are you going to do? He doesn't remember doing the deed, so it's gonna be kind of weird for you to tell him… Oh, man! You're gonna have to give him back his memories. What about his crew? Oh no! I always said that you were gonna get us killed! I haven't really lived yet. What is going to happen…" I grabbed her into a hug and whispered, "Don't worry, it will be okay. I promise you will survive. Please, just don't tell Mara, or let anyone from the crew pick your brain. This needs to go in that spot where you used to keep the location of your cash stash hidden from me. Remember?" I pulled away as she nodded so I continued, "I have a plan and I need both your and Mara's help." Right on cue, Mara chimed in, "You need our help with what?" I hadn't heard Mara return. I looked at her face to see if she had heard anything else, but she hadn't. I gave Thena a pleading look and she nodded once again. I guess she didn't trust herself to speak. "Well, I am sick of sitting here so I have a plan to get us out." Both Mara and Thena looked at me with hope in their eyes.

It was a farfetched plan, but anything was better than rotting in a small room, waiting for a miracle. I told them that and they both agreed. "Remember Great Aunt Ida?" Our Aunt Ida had been around for forever. She was our grandmother's sister and had to be about 100 years old, now. Our mother loved her aunt and although we didn't see her much, we loved her, too. As far as we knew, she was still alive. After they nodded, I continued, "Well, when Raknico came and told me that I was going to see you guys, he said something that made me think and connect some dots. That night, after a few hours of worrying, I had a dream about Aunt Ida. Well, she wasn't in the dream, my father was. He told me in my time of despair, she would shine light and provide answers to questions that plague me." They knew about all the dreams I had when I was younger and about how, whenever I dreamt about my father, the instructions he gave always pulled me from darkness. They've witnessed times in my life where the dreams came in handy, and I was hoping that they would trust me now. Mara looked at me expectantly, "So, what do you plan to do? Where do we fit in?" This plan was going to be hard on everyone, but it needed to be done. "I need you both to get as depressed as you can. Don't eat, don't sleep, cry. Do whatever you have to do to bring as much negative energy to this place. Try to get back to the place you were a few days ago. If they try to reunite us again, do not leave your room. If they somehow get you out of the room and together, pick fights with each other. I will send Raknico to each of you the night before he and I set off. After that, eat, sleep, and try to act normal." Mara held up her hand in confusion, "Wait, what does Raknico have to do with this?" Mara was always oblivious to connections between men and women. That's why I told her to date, so that she wouldn't end up an old maid. She may be doomed. I was looking a little worried that Thena would spill the beans. She gave me a reassuring smile and spoke, "Mara, how else was she gonna get out of this place? She can't very well just walk out." "Riiight!" Mara seemed to be satisfied with that answer. "I have a lot to do to um... persuade Raknico to take me, so give me, like, a week. In the meantime, try to focus all your positive energy on Raknico. My life depends on it. Oh, and don't let them get into your head... strong walls, please!"

We went back to talking about random things and reminiscing about our lives before this event. They allowed us to spend the whole day together, we laughed so much that when it was time to part, I almost broke in half. But I knew I had to stay strong for what came next.

CHAPTER TWELVE

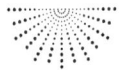

Keera

*I*t was late when I got back to my room. I finally had the will to shower, and maybe do something other than stare at the ceiling. I knew that the next time I saw Raknico, I would need to try to convince him of many things. I was just afraid that it would not go as smoothly as I would like it to.

I finished in the shower and stood in front of the bathroom mirror, staring at myself as I towel-dried my hair. I put on my sweats and headed to my room. I was actually looking forward to a good night's rest. I opened the bathroom door to exit when I was startled by Raknico sitting at my desk. "Good evening, Keera. I take it the gathering went well." Butterflies were flying all around my stomach as I tried to keep it light and calm, "As well as a day with my sisters could have gone. I missed them so much! Did the gathering go well for you and your crew?" I continued to stand in front of the bathroom door, twisting my drawstring around my finger, waiting for his reply.

"Ahh, indeed, they are feeling much better. Thank you for asking. I think we will need you to gather more often. It was a nice change to have some joy around here." He lowered his eyelids and studied me. My heart rate increased and I am sure it may have skipped a few beats. He stood up from the chair and took a step toward me. "There's something different about you tonight. Why is your heart beating like so? I've heard it change beat before, but this time it's much stronger. Why is that?" He continued to look at me like he was trying to probe me for answers. I was getting a little uncomfortable with the way he was staring at me. I knew he couldn't read my mind, but I wasn't sure if he could see what was going on with my body, so it was now or never. "Raknico, sit back down. There are things that you need to know... well, know again... because I need your help." He took another step forward, which caused me to increase some distance. "Raknico, please... this is important." He looked like he was weighing what I said then slowly stepped back and sat in the chair. "Keera, do share. Why is it that I need to know something... again? That would imply that I have forgotten. I never forget." I paced in front of him, trying to decide how I should tell him. I had to be delicate because I know this all will throw him for a loop. "Okay, you know how I occasionally ask you if you feel the spark?" He nodded and added, "Occasionally is an understatement. I feel you ask each time I see you." Waving my hand in dismissal, "That's beside the point. The reason I ask is because I want to see if you remember..." I gave a suggestive pause, "...us." I gave him a moment to let that sink in before I continued on. "You see, after we kissed, we star—" Jumping up, appalled, and almost knocking over the chair, Raknico said, "We did what!?" He looked disgusted and frightened. I took a deep breath, let it out slowly, and continued, "Well, something happened when we kissed and after that, we got close... like, real close. You catch my drift?" Looking back at me with mistrust, "Oh, I caught your drift, but I would never embark on anything relating to human relationships." I wasn't sure I could continue because of the revolted look on Raknico's face. He was making me feel like I was not something or someone capable of being loved. I gave him a moment to control his emotions. The room plummeted to below freezing. I wasn't sure how to handle this. In my head, my telling him about us would make him feel comfortable about accepting the pull we felt toward each other. Even without his memories, I felt like it would all happen the same as it did the first time around. I was completely wrong. I turned to sit on the bed. I pulled my knees to my chest and waited for Raknico to speak or leave. He paced in front of the bed. I could tell he wanted to say something, but he was holding back. I could tell that he had feelings of what felt like pain and joy. I had no clue as to where those feelings belonged. I was stumped.

He stopped pacing and faced me. "Okay, you said we kissed." I nodded. "How is it that I don't remember? I have never done that... umm," gesturing wildly with his hands, "... with a human before, so I think I would remember." He looked at me skeptically. Men; it doesn't matter who or what they are, they are always so concerned with their pride. It almost made me laugh that he was concerned that I would look at him differently if I knew he had never kissed anyone or anything before. It was my turn to educate him. "You don't remember because I locked your memories and only I have the key. You said that it was best if none of the crew could sense the change in you; that if you didn't remember the events, and the emotions along with them, we would be safe." He scoffed, "That's ridiculous! What change? Your story doesn't make sense. I am not going to sit here while some human tells me tales of her fantasies. You know..." The temperature in the room began to descend so, before he could continue, I panicked and couldn't prevent the words from spilling out, "We mated!" Raknico continued like he didn't hear me, or like he couldn't care less for what I said, "...all of this would imply some old ways of thinking on my part. I think we've seen enough of each other for a while. I will ask Saniyah to take over for me so that you can separate from some of your silly notions..." He continued speaking as he left the room but I stopped listening after "silly notions." This was going to be more difficult that I thought.

CHAPTER THIRTEEN

Raknico

I couldn't believe her… No, I wouldn't believe her! I know that I would never act in such an immodest way, especially when there is so much at stake. Where is my father when I need him? She was speaking preposterously. A mate! he scoffed. I've foreseen that I have a mate but that was on my planet, not here on Earth. This doesn't seem right. Me and Keera… mated? Where would I have found the time? What have I been doing these last few weeks? I think I've been studying my conversations with the human sisters. I had a meeting with Thena each day before lunch, Mara each day after lunch, and Keera each night after dinner. What else did I do with my time? I didn't rest much because I had so much pure energy pulsing through me. Come to think about it, I don't really recall a lot from the last few months. My days were filled with monotonous details. Keera said she locked my memories. Could it be that my father taught her the arts of the mind? She said that she did this at my request. Why would I think we wouldn't be safe? It would be the first relationship of its kind, in this century, at least. There had to be more to it. If she was telling the truth... oh no! What if she was telling the truth!? I could be mated to one not chosen by the High Appointed. Would that be the reason why I didn't think it was safe? Ahhh! So many questions and not enough answers. Deep down inside, I know that Keera is telling the truth. But I'm not sure I am ready for this level of truth yet.

Keera

My night was destroyed after Raknico stormed off. I didn't know what to do, so I cried. I didn't cry for too long because from within me, joy began to erupt. I didn't want to be happy. I wanted to cry until I fell asleep but, somehow, something was soothing me and willing me to let go of my grief. It succeeded, because I finally fell asleep without trouble and slept all night, without a touch of nightmares.

I began my morning like normal: staring at the ceiling. I no longer wanted to cry, which was weird because I still felt taken aback by Raknico's response. I heard the door open and a tray slip onto my desk. I didn't bother to put up my mental walls because I knew they only came to bring the tray of food. No one talked to me except for Raknico, and he probably wasn't coming back for a long time. I held back my tears because I had to start my day. I knew in order to keep my strength up I had to eat, so I slowly lifted my head from the pillow. I didn't bother to open my eyes just yet. I knew they were swollen and red from crying last night. I stretched my arms above my head. I opened my eyes to yawn but cut it short when I noticed that Saniyah was standing by the door, looking at me. I gave her a smile and greeted her, "Good morning, Saniyah." She mimicked my smile and sat in my desk chair. "Raknico sent me to look after you." My heart leapt at the sound of his name. "I did not understand his request, but I do follow orders." She looked me up and down. "There's something different. You are…" I gave her my best poker face, then raised one of my eyebrows. I think she could sense my inner turmoil, but I didn't want to make things easier for her. I put up my mental blocks and I pushed her probes away from me. Since I was revealing some of my abilities, I tried to send her some of my energy as well; I could use the practice. It was incredibly easy to do. She looked at me, surprised. "But… how? How are you doing that? You are not one of us. I… I… you…" I nodded my head to agree. "I know. You don't know the half of it." I walked away, signaling the end of the conversation. I went into the bathroom to shower. I stood under the flow of the water. *I'm different; what did she mean?* I wanted to know exactly what she meant, but I didn't want her getting too nosy. This was just getting too confusing and hard to maneuver on my own. Why did Raknico refuse to believe me and come back so that we could work this out together? I felt so alone and before I knew it, I was crying… again. I don't have or know anyone to talk to about this. My sisters would never understand what I am going through. My father was my voice of reason, and he's not here. At that thought, I started crying harder. What does the future have in store for me? I just hoped that Raknico got it together before I fell completely apart. I stayed in the shower until my skin ridges were plump with wrinkles. Saniyah was gone when I got out the shower. I was glad because I didn't want to be confronted about what she heard from the bathroom, or about me being different. I had dual emotions running through my body. I knew I was different because my father told me as much, but she sees something else and that's where my curiosity peaked. I sat at the desk to eat my meal mechanically, while my mind swirled with thoughts. When I finished, I laid in the bed and forced myself to go to sleep, and to hopefully avoid any confrontations with Saniyah.

CHAPTER FOURTEEN

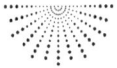

Two days later...

Keera

I found myself crying for days. I didn't know that a person could continuously cry for days, but I proved the theory. I went through cycles of joy and pain. I would start crying, and then feel peace. When I thought about Raknico and the hope he brought, I would start to cry again. After the first confrontation with Saniyah, I slept until late in the evening. I woke to find that my breakfast tray had been taken away and replaced with a dinner tray. I ate what was left for me and went back to sleep. I am sure that it was Saniyah that brought my meals, and I wouldn't put it past her to stand over my sleeping body and try to figure me out. Each morning I would wake to Saniyah standing at the door, and my breakfast tray sitting on the desk. It made me uncomfortable that she just stood there and stared at me. I wondered if she has been successful in breaking down my mental walls. I would have to be sure to fortify my walls before sleep each night. I was done with the scrutiny, so I began hiding myself. I would walk to the bathroom to brush my teeth, then walk past Saniyah, pick up the tray, then take it to the bathroom to eat. After each time I finished, I would exit the bathroom and she would be gone. This went on for all meals. With each meal that Saniyah brought me, she looked more and more sad and sympathetic toward me. Although a part of me wanted to know the meaning behind her expressions, I couldn't care less about how she viewed me. After eating a meal, I always retreated to the bed for a forced nap. I would put up strong walls, but I could feel my will failing. My world was crumbling around me, and I didn't know how to save it.

Raknico

The reports that Saniyah was giving me were getting worse as time went on. Keera was not doing well and I felt it was my fault. Why couldn't I just believe her and allow her to unlock the memories that I didn't believe were locked? From that first day Saniyah was on duty, she shared her memories of what occurred. Saniyah could sense something different about Keera. Why couldn't I? I may have allowed my confusion and denial to fog up my senses. Keera must have been careless, because she allowed Saniyah to experience some of her abilities no human should possess. Even in this memory, I could sense that Keera was getting stronger at a fast rate.

Saniyah now knows there is something special about Keera. I didn't elaborate, but I knew that I would have to be open with Saniyah, sooner rather than later. For now, I would keep what I knew to myself, and trust that she would not tell another soul what she knows.

After seeing Keera spend that first day crying, I knew I had to look within myself and find some truth. It was apparent that Keera believed and, based on how she has been doing, I had to trust that the truth was also within. It took some time, and a large amount of effort, but I found the locked place in my mind. I tried all that I could to unlock them, but to no avail. I expended my energy reserves and had to sleep for an extended period to revive myself after attempting to unlock the place in my mind. This proved that she was telling the truth. I am so flawed. I should have done this right at the start. Something had occurred between us, and it was important enough for me to instruct her to hide the memories. My father taught her well. No one could penetrate those walls. I felt proud. It was like a dark cloud lifted off me and I was finally able to see straight. I'm mated! How is this possible, when the mating ceremony could not possibly be performed? Oh, Grand Father, I needed to find out what happened within those gaps in my mind. Without it, I don't know the type of danger she... no, we, could be in.

Keera

It was evening once again and I woke to a tantalizing aroma. Looking around the room, I ensured I was alone, before getting up and lazily walking to the desk. I took off the tray cover and noticed that it was my favorite Italian dish – Baked Rigatoni Pomodoro. *How did they know?* There is no way they picked my brain to find this. Saniyah didn't even skim the surface of my mind. This smelled like a deep apology. *Raknico.* Excitement coursed through me until I remembered he had no memory of us and, therefore, was not likely to care. With that thought, I instantly stilled. I sat down at the desk and breathed in the great smell. I began to shovel food into my mouth, caring less and less about the reason with each passing bite. I hummed while I ate it, savoring the greatness of fine Italian flavors. It was so delicious! I finished the meal in no time, leaving behind nothing but a clean plate. I went to the bathroom to wash my hands, continuing the happy hum exploding from my core. I added a little dance, while I washed. "I see that you have enjoyed your dinner." I stopped humming and froze. I inhaled deeply and found his scent. Raknico smelled of sandalwood, lavender, and morning dew. He always smelled inviting, but he was putting my senses in hyperdrive right now. He continued, despite my silence, "It was not easy to get." I continued to wash my hands, pushing my excitement deeper. I didn't want him to think that he would be forgiven that fast. "Well, congratulations, I see you know how to order takeout." It wasn't confirmed that we were still in my hometown, or if we were even still on Earth, but with food like that, we had to still be Earth-bound. When I finished drying my hands, I squeezed my way between him and the door frame. He was posted in the doorway, looking so delicious. *What is wrong with me? I never objectify men.* I smiled to myself. *That was Thena's forte.* "Please, Keera, look at me." His plea was heartfelt. His apology came rushing through me but I just did not want to be disappointed again. Angry heat rose in my blood and I snapped my head up, "Look, Raknico, I don't have time for this. You have already expressed how you feel about this lowly human." I sent my coldness back at him as I pointed to myself. The words sliced through my heart. I turned away from him. I knew I was more than that, but it still didn't dismiss that we were put on the lowest caste level.

He took a deep breath and exhaled. "You are more than that. I was just upset and taking it out on you. Please look at me." That was something I could not accept. I pushed all my emotions at him, feeling satisfied when I heard him grunt in pain. "You had no reason to be angry with me. I just needed you to know. I needed support. I have no one, since you and your crew took away my sisters. Give me one reason why I should even give you the satisfaction of looking you in the eye?" An additional reason unspoken in my impatient stance. He approached me and pressed his chest against my back. Upon contact, there was a flash of light that was a spectrum of colors. The electric shock went through my body and fizzled all around us. I gasped and he sighed. "Because I do feel the spark when we touch." I turned to face him and looked into his pained eyes. "It is new for me and, as far as I know, none of our people have ever experienced it." He was suffering and looked confused. I put my hand on his cheek, "You believe me?" He brought his hand up to wipe away a tear that I didn't know I had shed. "I do. I found a locked place in my mind. But not just that. I've felt the spark from the first moment we touched in your home. There was something there from the start." We stared into each other's eyes for a minute, caressing each other's hands, enjoying the sensation. It was a low hum that filled my whole body with climactic satisfaction. My eyes met his lips and my body began to follow my gaze. He stepped away, looking sheepish and downright delicious. *Here we go again.* "I don't know how to be with a... human." I smiled at him and used my hand to guide his head so that our eyes met. "I can unlock your memories and you will see that you do know." I could feel his nervousness. "I mean, if you want me to. Are you ready for that?" I could feel that he was still unsure, but he nodded. I took his hand and led him to the bed, turning him to sit. He hesitated, but sat and turned toward me. I sat next to him and placed my hands on top of his. I closed my eyes and began unlocking the past.

Raknico

I closed my eyes and focused on what Keera was doing. I opened my mind's eye and found myself being drawn out of the present and into a white room. Everything was white: the walls, floor, ceiling. It was like I was in a room where nothing else existed. In the distance, there was something fast approaching. Warning bells went off and I searched for an escape. There was nothing I could do to stop what was coming for me, so I closed my eyes tightly and braced for impact.

It hit me right in the face with a force that should have knocked me down. I gasped, which forced me to open my eyes, where I saw this object going into me. I looked closely and saw that they were images. The images were coming from the locked place in my mind. The lock was gone, so I opened the door. The white started to fade and I found myself standing in Keera's room, watching her... with me. It was surreal. I went over to wave my hand in front of my face and nothing happened. I tried to touch Keera's face and my hand went straight through it. This was amazing memory recall. *She's amazing.* It reminded me of a holographic viewing -- part of the scene, but only as an observer.

Keera and I continued with our conversation. Keera quickly waved her arms about. The timeline came to me. It was the day Shanluk almost expired. *I don't remember going to her room after I teleported Shanluk out.* I was asking her for details. I watched very closely. I saw myself place a hand on each of her arms and felt as an electric charge surged through my body. *What was that?* It felt absolutely heavenly. I closed my eyes and moaned in pleasure. I opened them again and saw the shock and pleasure registering on my face in the scene; we all felt the strength of the touch. It was the greatest feeling I have ever felt in my existence. I continued to watch. We stared into each other's eyes, not making a move. *MINE.* Suddenly the events moved in a faster than normal pace. We kissed, then the picture faded away. I was then hit again with a moving object and my body was given more memories...

...I enter her room with lust on my mind. *LUST!* My people are not physical. I don't know where these feelings are coming from. She is sitting at the desk reading a book. She looks up at me and smiles. I move across the room like a predator and she stands up in anticipation. I smash into her and we begin to kiss, I feel so many things at this moment: there is a buildup of electricity centered in my chest from fear and excitement. I back away from her to catch my breath. The buildup disappears quickly and my reason for visiting comes back to me. I question her about my Father. She beams when she remembers him.

"He kept the dark away. He told me I was special. He also brought out my abilities and said that he had to prepare me for something big. I never did get into much detail about that 'something big', but before he left, he said that I was ready."

Ready for what?

...

...We are lying in Keera's bed. Both of our pulses are racing and we are breathing heavily. We are fully clothed but our clothes are wrong and improperly placed. *I look... different.* I cannot believe I am in casual clothes and not my flight suit. Keera begins speaking, so I listen in.

"I dreamed of my father before I met him. I didn't know it was him at first. I was young and he told me he was my grand-father." She laughs. "I was so young! Now that I think about it, I believe he said, 'I am called The Grand Father.' I just thought he meant he was my grandfather." I join in the humor of Grand Father presenting himself. "Anyway, he was just a voice in my dreams, at first, then he gradually became more real. The first time we met in person, he spoke and he was familiar, but I couldn't place him." Confusion etched my face, "Place him?" She waves her hand. "Oh, it just means I felt like I met him but couldn't remember from where." She laughs again. "He told my mom that he was the new guidance counselor." She doubles over in laughter. I am unsure of why he lied to her mother, but it was for a good reason, I'm sure. "Something he said clicked and then I remembered he was from my dreams." She smiles like I do when I think of Grand Father. "I fell in love and called him father." ...

… Again, we are lying on Keera's bed. My shirt is off and she is lying over my chest, tracing my symbols. "Father said that this is your history, but no one has been able to translate the language, is that still true?" I nodded. "It's amazing how they appear, disappear, then reappear in a different place." She traced the symbol that resembled the human Celtic symbol, the Eternal Knot. I inhale, sucking the air through my teeth. "Can you feel that?" Sultry curiosity laced her voice. "I can." She continues to trace the symbols. "It feels very erotic to have you trace the symbols. I have never felt this before. We are not allowed to touch on my planet. It is considered one of the entryways to the Beneath. Physical contact was banned because there are too many factors in it that lead people to feel emotions like hate and jealousy. I always thought love and physical affection were the strongest of positive energy. The High Appointed saw them as risks, and they were banned long ago. Even before my father became Grand Father," I finish in a whisper, then lay quietly to reflect. Keera touches my hand, snapping me back into the moment. "That's so sad. I don't know what I would do if I couldn't be hugged, or if I couldn't kiss you. Sometimes words fail and the only thing to do is hold someone until they find the positive side to life." …

… I arrive as both Keera and I are emerging from under the sheets. I inhale the mixed scent. We had just committed the ultimate act of love. I look upon us with amazement. We wear satisfied grins across our sweat-beaded faces. We are panting and staring into each other's eyes as if we are in a trance. We glisten from the sweat, and a layer of electricity that is flowing around us. We move closer and press our heads together, like gravity drew us in. The electricity flowing around us seems to quicken, then absorb into our bodies, darkening the room. The darkness closes around me as the silence grows. When it feels as if the darkness will devour me, I hear movement and deep moaning. I do not know what is going on. I close my eyes to focus. I can feel pleasure seeping through every cell of my body. The core of my chest begins to heat up. Electricity slowly rises within that heat. I am not afraid. Keera is touching me. *MINE.* I can feel the sensation of her hands and body against mine, as well as if they were my hands and my body doing the touching. I am moving inside her, as well. We match rhythms, so I can't tell where she ends and where I begin, not that it matters. The electricity intensifies and when we reach the highest level of rapture, the electricity explodes, illuminating the room. I have to close my eyes to shield them from the assaulting light. When I open them again, the scene speeds up, then slows.

We were lying on the bed, looking at each other in amazement. It was the same night and the room was still blindingly bright. *I felt... different.* My head was full of thoughts that did not belong to me. It was strange, because I could feel thoughts from Keera and I as we lay on the bed but I can now feel Keera, just out of reach, worrying about me. I blocked enough to focus, and looked onto the scene in front of me. "We... mated? Does that mean we're married?" I couldn't hide my smirk, "It's deeper than that but, essentially, we are married. How you say: 'Til death do us part.'" Keera looked stunning, even in a state of shock. "So, you're saying we mated! How do you know? You said it yourself that physical contact has been banned. If no one in your world mates anymore, how does one marry or have children? Are we in trouble?" There was trembling in her voice and tears forming in her eyes. I pulled her close. "No one has "mated" in this way for at least a century. Since the physical contact was causing people to be tainted by less than neutral energy, mating occurred less and less. Less people mated, and fewer children were brought into the world. When the High appointed declared physical contact illegal, mating disappeared, and our people started to suffer." *That's horrible.* I laugh out of excitement from being able to hear Keera in my head. "It was. With no one mating the traditional way, we didn't have children being born, so there was not enough pure energy flowing to keep people healthy and alive." I felt Keera's sadness flow through me. "It was then the High Appointed, under the direction of the Grand Father of that time, decided that we needed to find other methods of reproducing and mating. They created a mating song that can only be sung in notes heard in our atmosphere. Once the song is complete, the two people are as one." *What about kids?* The question rang in my head, as if knowing what my next words would be. "It is with that song that children are conceived, though I do not know the specifics behind that." She put her hand to her mouth, heat rising to her cheeks. "Oh." I continued, "Also, different from us, they cannot hear each other's thoughts and emotions. But they depend on each other's life force to survive. If one expires, so does the other." We sit while Keera takes it all in. "What about us?" I pondered the question a short while before answering, "Well, I honestly don't know for sure. I know we hear each other's thought and emotions. It's like we became one being. I believe we depend on each other's life force, so your lifespan is considerably longer, now that you are tapping into my life force."

We hold each other tighter. A dark thought crosses my mind, causing Keera to flinch in my arms. "We should use caution, though. Guard your thoughts and emotions in front of others until I know for sure." She nods…

… We are again lying in the bed. Our bodies once again heated, electrified, and beading with sweat. We are in each other's arms, enjoying our quiet conversation between thoughts. I am watching a memory of a dream. "What is this?" I look at her, curious about the dream. She shrugged her shoulders. "Oh, I don't know. It's a recurring dream I have. I told my mom about it once, and Father overheard. He asked my mom to get her something from the kitchen and when she left the room, he said that dream was the reason he was here. He said I was an important piece in the future of his people. I didn't understand."

I still don't understand.

"I'm just standing on some mountain, touching some glowing object. I never understood the importance." I sat up in the bed. "Do you see anyone else there?" She shrugs her shoulders again. "Not really. I can only see the light that's coming from that object. I feel safe, but everything else is blurry." She looks at me with wide eyes. "Why are you acting so strange?" I just look at her and push a thought to her. It was of myself, standing on that same mountain, in front of that same glowing object. She gasped. "That is a dream that I have, and have had since I was a young boy. I have never told anyone but Grand Father. I have other recurring dreams, but this one feels the strongest. Like… I have …"

"…the weight of the world on your shoulders."

Keera finished my sentence. It is so weird to be so in sync, but magical at the same time. It is unheard of for both our cultures. An idea sparks… more like a memory. A story my father would tell me whenever I had the dream. Remembering those moments, I begin to recite the verse aloud:

"Like-minded beings of two different worlds come together as one. The Legacy and Destiny are related strangers that, through energy and forgotten pasts, create the purest immortal power known to the galaxy. Ending the carnivorous reign, their powers bring forth the future."

A familiar coolness hit me in my bones. "It makes sense. We are made for each other. I mean, we mated, so that means our souls knew their mate. Is that why my father would recite that after I had that dream? He did say Keera was important to the future of our race… I wonder…" Keera tapped my arm and looked at me quizzically. "Father used to recite that to me all the time. I thought it was a spell or something, because I would feel weird after. You think that's us? It sounds like we are supposed to save the world."

No way. She snickers, then stops when she sees I'm just staring at her. "Are we supposed to save the world?"

I feel the panic rise in her heart. "My love, don't worry. There is a reason for all things. If we are meant to save the world, it means we have the power to make it happen. I just don't know how… yet."

…

… I rushed into Keera's room. She could sense that it was me.

"I wasn't expecting you yet," she turned and noticed my

expression. "Keera, I can't hide how I feel for you. You have been doing wonderfully, but I feel like I was not created to hide my love."

She took me into an embrace. "Nico, we will make it work. We will find a way. You need to practice your mental walls and your emotion—"

"I cannot! I love you and it is giving me the purest energy I have ever known. Kemorte is onto me and he is dark. I fear he will fall, or worse yet, try to drain you of your heavenly energy, starving me to death. You have to do something. Please. I don't want to lose you." I could feel my stress as my mind sought out all the bad scenarios. The vulnerability in myself shocked me. I also felt Keera's fear of being drained and losing me. "What do we do?" Although I have already thought about what needed to be done, I paused for effect before answering. "Remember when you told me that my father taught you the art of manipulating the mind?" I waited until she caught on. Her eyes grew and her voice lowered, "You want me to mess with your brain! Are you crazy!?" I lowered my voice, "I'm not crazy. I'm just worried about what could happen if the wrong people found out." I could sense her reluctance. "Look, this will be temporary. Just know that I love you and when the time is right, talk to me and make me remember." She nodded and wrapped her arms around me tighter, like she was never going to hug me again. *Oh no. Keera.* I couldn't stop feeling the deep sadness dripping from Keera. I pulled away from the memories, allowing them to just continue flowing through me, making me whole again. I closed my eyes and focused on my breathing. It won't be long before I am ready to greet my mate and tell her I love her.

Keera

I kept my eye on Raknico while he laid on the bed with his eyes closed. He was unmoving and in deep meditation. I knew he was processing the memories, and the emotions behind them. I had never locked anyone's memories before, so I didn't know what to expect. He was still breathing. *Thank God for that.* Father taught me this skill, as in instructed me on how to perform it, but I never had the opportunity to use it. I just hope that I didn't injure him. I pray that he recovers soon. I do not want to have to drag someone in from the crew and face the repercussions.

I had finished unlocking the memories and, for what seemed like hours, I kept vigil. I was at my wits' end. I got up to pace, then decided it was time to call Saniyah. Just as my hand came up to bang on the door, Raknico gasped and woke from his meditation.

I stepped closer to him. "Raknico... Nico. Are you okay?" He sat up, swinging his legs off the bed with his head bent low. He dropped to the floor on his knees in front of me. He reached for me, grabbed me around my waist, and pulled me close, into a hug. "My mate... My beautiful mate!" My body shook as tears fell. It was finally coming together. He had successfully remembered our time together. He pulled away from me to stand. He kissed my tears and then kissed my lips with so much passion. My knees almost gave out, but I stayed standing so that I could continue the kiss. Raknico ran his hands along my arms. He brought his hands up to my neck. He remembered it all. I felt my pulse quicken, then he broke the kiss. He led me to the bed to sit. We sat down and began kissing again. His hands were all over my body. The electricity was flowing through my body at such speeds, I thought I was going to burst. He pulled my shirt over my head. Instead of waiting until my head was free from the shirt, he began kissing my chest, moving further and further down, to the top of my pants. He grabbed the elastic band of my sweatpants and pulled them down. I felt so exposed. It had been a few weeks of him treating me like a stranger that made me feel like it was the first time all over again. He sensed my thought.

"Keera, you are beautiful and, tonight, I will make up for that time we were not able to be together."

He got off the bed and slipped out of his flight pants. He knelt on the floor and, at the angle I was lying, he disappeared. I began to prop myself up on my elbows when I was dragged to the edge of the bed. I let out a surprised scream, then laughed and lay back down. He began pleasuring me with his beautiful mouth. He may not have been born into a world where there is much physical contact, but he was made for physical intimacy. At last, the electricity pulsing through my body exploded toward the ceiling. I lay there panting. Raknico laid with me and we curled together in each other's arms, without a care in the world. I was satiated and didn't want to move, but there was no time to waste. I had to tell him about the plan so that we could be safe. Raknico began kissing my neck. I could feel my pulse quickening all over again. Before I could let him move any further, I put my hand on his chest. *I don't want to stop.*

"Nico, we have to find my Aunt Ida. She taught Father that poem. Father wanted me to go to her. She can help us answer the questions we have about the dream and the verse." He let out a pained breath. "And don't ask me how I know. I just do."

He repositioned himself and brought me to his chest. I could hear the rhythmic beating of his heart. We waited until the electricity settled before talking. From the echoes of his chest cavity I could hear him speak. "Tell me what needs to be done and I will do it." I told him the plan I had concocted with my sisters, and he told me that he would take care of the rest. We lay in each other's arms awhile before our lips found each other again.

CHAPTER FIFTEEN

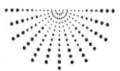

Keera

*I*t wasn't such a difficult thing to pull off. Thena and Mara did a wonderful job of acting depressed. I guess it wasn't a hard thing to do, since everything around us made us depressed. The crew was so weak from my sisters' depression, that they hadn't sensed the change in the energy from Raknico and I. They didn't have an opportunity to probe into our changes. They were so busy with trying to survive the depressive wave. *Sorry, not sorry.* After I told Raknico that I asked my sisters to starve the crew of positive energy so that we would get a chance to run away, he kissed me so passionately that I almost forgot where I was.

He thought it was great thinking on my toes, even when I didn't have him to back me. I reassured him that I was not trying to starve them to death, but only make them so delirious that they wouldn't notice our disappearance or change, due to the mating. He was onboard with no questions asked, and I was pleased at his turn around. I told him where my Aunt's house was. He gave me a map of my town so that I could point it out. He planned to teleport us there, so as not to waste time. I was not sure how the plan would work, but I trusted him with my life.

On the day of our departure, he left to go do his rounds with my sisters. He was going to update them on the plan, and run drills with them to test the strength of their mental walls. I knew they would need the practice, but it was the middle of the night before he returned to the room. He entered my room and approached me. I had been ready and set to go for hours, but didn't complain. I didn't have much to take with me so when he entered the room, I was packed to go. He instead pulled me close and bent down to kiss me, like he was never seeing me again. I panicked at that thought. Sensing my stress, Raknico pulled away and looked at me. "You know, we don't have to do this. We can find another way." I shook my head, "No, we have to go. I need to go. It's what Father would have wanted."

Raknico smiled, nodded, and grabbed me by the waist. "This may feel a little strange." He pushed a button on his suit. Before I had a chance to respond, we shifted out of the room. We appeared on the street in front of my aunt's house. Raknico held me up, trying to make sure I could stand straight. I pulled away to look at my aunt's house. "I could have told you that I have teleported before." I detached myself and turned to take the house in. "Look at that house. Still looks the same."

I stood there, admiring the house. It was an old ranch in the middle of the woods. I believe the house used to be white, but with age and the greenery growing on the sides, you wouldn't be able to tell. It stood tall and proud, as if it had a personality. It was the perfect house for my aunt. She loved nature! She said that the natural world was the purest part of the world and that any time you needed rejuvenation, the woods was the place to do it. It was true; I felt better standing there, just at the border of the woods.

Raknico walked up and stood next to me, close enough that I felt the electric surge. "Ready?" I took his hand as he led me to the house. The lights were on, so I knew my aunt was home. I was nervous. I hope she remembers me, and I hope that she knows why my Father would send me to her. There was only one way to find out, so we began to approach the house.

CHAPTER SIXTEEN

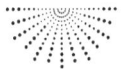

Keera

$\mathcal{W}$e walked slowly to the house, like we were walking to our death. We arrived at the porch and I took a deep breath. I looked up at Raknico, searching his eyes for strength. His face softened and was all the encouragement I needed. I brought up my hand and knocked on the old wooden door. I could hear someone walking around inside. The floorboards creaked as they got closer and closer to the front door. The lock clicked back and the door slowly opened, with the door chain still in place, revealing a small woman with white hair.

"Hi. May I help you?"

"Aunt Ida, it's me, Keera. I was told to come to you. My father sent me."

She just stared back, squinting her eyes. She opened the door slightly wider to get a look at Raknico. She looked up and down, raising an eyebrow. A spot of recognition crossed her face and she lit up. "Is it that time already!?" She closed the door and unhooked the chain to open the door wider. "Please, child, come in. I've been waiting for y'all." She swung the door open and walked toward the back of the house. I looked to Raknico and mouthed: *She's been waiting for us?* He just shrugged his shoulders and took the lead into the house.

Aunt Ida was nowhere to be found. We looked around at all the antiques around her small ranch. The color was so dull, due to the fact that the walls hadn't seen new paint in years. "Y'all have a seat in the living room. Please, make yourselves at home." We looked around and found the room that resembled a living room to our left. We tentatively walked into the room, around all the newspapers and breakable heirlooms. We found the couch under papers yellowed with age. I never recalled my aunt's home looking this way. Upon sitting, I shouted back, "What did you mean by 'you've been waiting for us?' How did you know we'd come?" I heard banging noises that sounded like she was in the kitchen, looking for some cookware to use. "Y'all want some tea?" I quickly responded, letting her know we weren't thirsty. I wanted her to come in and answer some questions, so that we could go on our merry way and know for sure that we were not supposed to save the world.

Aunt Ida shuffled in a few minutes later, with a handful of dishes and a pot full of tea. We watched her struggle with the tray. Raknico stood to help her, but was waved away, and ordered to sit down. She said something to the effect of, 'I'm stronger than I look', but didn't say it clearly enough to be fully heard. She placed the tray down on what looked like the coffee table, in front of us. She looked up and smiled. "Well,

Keera, get up! Let me take a look at you." I stood hesitantly. "You grew up to be a beautiful woman. You look just like your momma." I smiled at that, but the smile quickly faded away. I missed my mother. Sensing the reason for my sadness, she grabbed my hands and gave them a squeeze. "No worries, child. You're mother would never leave you of her own free will. Trust that there is a plan, and at the end of the journey, all will be clear." It was very cryptic, but I just smiled and gave her hands a return squeeze.

She walked over to Raknico, motioning him to stand. She cupped his face. "Ahh, you look just like your father. Strong like him, too, I suppose." Raknico and I exchanged looks. "You knew my father?" Aunt Ida waved her hand. "Knew? I know your father. I was actually part of the High Appointed when he asked me to perform a special task." She sat down in the chair across from us and continued. "It was my job to find the one spoken about in the prophecy. See, no one but the Grand Father and the High Appointed knew the truth behind the prophecy... well, what we thought was the truth." She laughed, then coughed. "Anyway, I was sent here to find the one mentioned in the prophecy. See, my visions are not always clear. I couldn't see faces or places, but I could sense when I was at the right place at the right time. It took me ages to find the right place. Then it was time for me to watch for the right time."

She sat back, allowing what she had uncovered to be absorbed. Finally, it dawned on me. "Wait... so, you're not my great aunt? You are someone from another planet, who posed as a member of my family?" I was somewhat hurt by this notion. I didn't have much family left, and those that I did have seemed to be lessening in numbers faster and faster these days. She gave me a sympathetic smile. "I am not your aunt as you believed. I am from another place. It was not our plan to hurt or harm you. I was just supposed to get close enough to whoever was mentioned in the prophecy. I tried many ways, and the only way to make it work was to integrate myself into your family. I do apologize for the pain that it has caused you." Raknico squeezed my hand. I felt more at ease by his side.

Aunt Ida, or whoever she was, looked at us with dignity. "I am Idava, the High Appointed Seeker and oracle for the Vaehte people." She performed a small bow. Something registered in Raknico's eyes. "I remember stories of you. They said that you fell from grace. You were known as 'The Dark Queen!' How is that you came here?" She let out a belly laugh, "Well, I am definitely NOT the Queen of the Beneath! That job is reserved for someone else. As you can see, I did not fall. I simply moved through space." I shook my head. "Wait. Just. One. Minute. How can this be? You were my aunt. I mean, I have many memories of you, and so do my mother and sisters. How long have you been here? Have you aged much?" *You look the same.* "Child, everything is not what it seems. I have been here for some time and I age at a different rate than you. As for your memories, I planted them or placed myself in the memories that you and your family members had. It had to be done; you are chosen to save our world." Panic swelled in me. "So, it's true. We ARE supposed to save the world. How do we do that? I mean, I know of that verse and it says that we come together. Well…" I felt heat in my cheeks. "We've already come together. How come that hasn't saved your world?" Idava looks at me and clicks her tongue against her teeth, "Keera, there is more to that "verse" than just the mating." I blushed even more as she spoke. "Listen to what's between the words." She began to recite the verse again. When she spoke, I felt the air stirring and a chill resting on both Raknico and I. We stood up, surveying the change. I looked at him, "You feel it, too?" He simply nodded and looked back to Idava. She came close to us and grabbed our free hands. "Children, you are meant for greater things." She looked at Raknico, "Son, you are meant to lead. Lead our people into the future of change." She then turned to look back to me, "Keera, you paved the way for Raknico. You are the reason he can bring about change. You…" Idava let go of my hand and placed it at my stomach. "… and what's growing inside of you, are what will change AND save the world." My mouth gaped open. I couldn't believe my ears. She was telling me that I was pregnant, and this baby was the power that would save the world. I couldn't speak. I heard voices from afar but couldn't bring myself to the present. I was afraid: afraid of being a mother, of saving the world. I still had no clue as to how it would get done. Motherhood was a feat all by itself. I felt the hot sting of tears rolling down my face. *Mommy, I need you.*

I registered someone's hand wiping them away. "Keera! Are you okay?" The voice became louder as I came back to the present. The drum of my heart became faint as my vision came into focus. Raknico was wiping my tears away and asking me questions. "Keera, are you okay? Do you need to sit? I can't believe this! I'm so happy!" I knew he was. I felt it through every cell of my body. I was happy, too, but my fear took the front seat. I closed my eyes, put my hand to my stomach, and focused. It was there. This little tiny person was there, and for some reason I think I already knew. *Ours.* I smiled and continued to cry. It was a blessing. Anything this good could not fail. Even if I had no clue how, I had the strength and courage to do it. When I finally stopped and opened my eyes, Idava was nowhere to be found. I looked at Raknico and saw his beaming smile. He looked back at my face, while gesturing to my stomach. "May I?" I nodded. His hands went to my stomach and he closed his eyes. He held them closed for a minute, then smiled. He opened his eyes and knelt to kiss my stomach. He stood and gave me a quick kiss. "He is so strong already! I could feel him, separate from you." I was shocked. "How do you know it's a boy?" He smiled, then kissed me again. "I don't. I am just hopeful!" We both laughed. *How had we missed him?* We sat down and Raknico held me in his arms.

Idava walked back into the room after giving us a moment to digest the information. "That verse, as you call it, is a prophecy. The only prophecy that is imperative to our future. If it goes unfulfilled, there are other prophecies that will come into action, and they all signal the end of our world."

No pressure.

I could feel the exasperation rise within me, "Well, everything is put into motion. What else do we have to do to save the world? Nico and I use our powers, and the power of the child, to save the world? I don't get it!" I put my fingers to my temple and closed my eyes. "You are the key to the future, but you have to be in the right place, and in the right time to fulfill it. You know where that is. You both have seen it."

The dream.

Raknico and I both came to the realization at the same

time. We remembered that we both shared a dream in which we could not see any other person, but we could see a great power in front of us. I turned to Raknico and focused on him. I could feel that he was doing the same. I don't know why I never thought to look into his dream. I found it, and it was like we were looking at the same scene. I blended our memories of our dreams. Now I could see that he was standing opposite me, reaching out to the same bright glowing object. Then I heard it, crying. It was a baby. We were reaching out and we were touching our baby. This was madness, but so beautiful. Idava stood in front of us, breaking us out of our trance with her voice so startlingly close, "That's right, children. The legend is that the chosen will know the way to saving the world. I knew the 'who' but the where and when was beyond my vision. Now, you both know the 'who' and 'where'. The 'when' will reveal itself when the time is here." I was still a little confused, "But I don't know where this takes place. I've never seen this place before." Raknico smiled, "No worries, my mate. I know exactly where it is." Pride filled his voice, "That is Mount Appointed. That is where the High Counsel hold meetings, perform mating ceremonies, and perform what you may call in-vitro fertilization. That is my home." My head was spinning. "Aunt Ida, I'll have that tea now."

CHAPTER SEVENTEEN

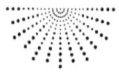

Keera

I sat there, sipping my tea, trying to make sense out of everything. Idava left us, once again, to our own thoughts. We got answers, but those answers only led to more questions. She returned with a disc in hand. "I also have something to show y'all." She placed the disc down. "Before The Grand Father left, he gave me this disc to give to you both. I already know the contents, so I will leave you to it." She walked away without another word. Of course, she didn't want to watch it with us. She probably saw it before Father gave it to her to keep. Raknico and I stared at the disc. It was nothing I had ever seen. Raknico picked it up. "I have seen these, but only in museums."

"What is it? It looks like a disc, but not one that would play in a DVD or CD player; some weird computer disc?"

"An interactive holographic disc." He did not elaborate. I guessed what it would do because of its name. It was technology that was beyond what we had, so I know it had to have come from his planet. Raknico moved the disc like he knew what he was doing. The disc was smaller than a DVD, but larger than one of the mini discs. It was dark silver on the outer ring and the inner solid ring, where the hole would be, was of lighter silver. There was no writing or label to help decipher which way was up. It did have symbols moving on it, so it had to be older than this century or so. He sat it down and pressed the lighter silver. Although it did not depress like a button, the center acted like a play button and the outer part of that center began to glow a golden color. It began to glow upward, to form a picture. It was a hologram of my father. He started to speak:

"Greetings, Raknico and Keera. I imagine there are many questions running through your minds and you don't have enough answers to cover them. I apologize for not being able to be more upfront with you, but I did it this way to safeguard your thoughts and emotions. You are the chosen, and I did all I could to prepare you for your destiny. The knowledge you possess now is enough to move forward. You will fill in the gaps as you go. I fear I have unfortunate news." Raknico and I looked at each other.

"There is a dark energy rising. As you now know, Idava is not the Dark Queen as has been rumored...but please remember, the Dark Queen does exist. It seems that whoever she is, she has found someone to rule with her and bring about the destruction of our world. Beware of the dark energy. You will know the energy I speak of when you encounter it. You need to stop this energy from killing our world. Raknico, protect your mate. For without her, all is lost. I'm proud of you, both of you. Congratulations and good luck!" The image disappeared. My fear must have been written on my face because Raknico grabbed me and brought me close to his chest. "It will be okay, my mate. I will not fail us." I didn't respond. It was not him that I was afraid would fail. I was afraid I would fail, and their world would end.

Raknico

The message from my father was unnerving, but I had to be strong for Keera. I knew she feared failure and I had to do everything in my power to not allow us to fail. My father said to protect her and our unborn child. I will do that until the last ounce of my life force is depleted. I can't believe, in all these years, my father knew I was the chosen. How had I not seen it? Now that I really listen to the verse, it had always been me. I was Legacy because I was heir to the throne, and Keera was Destiny. I had to laugh at myself because now it made sense. In my native tongue, Keera is spelled k-i-y-r-u-h-e and that, translated, would mean 'destiny'. I never made the connection before. Though it is spoken the same way, the meaning separates and confirms the validity of the prophecy. It has also gotten me curious as to who wrote the prophecy. I never knew name of the oracle that preceded Idava. It would have been nice to know her history. Now that we know that Idava is not the Dark Queen, we need to figure out who the Dark Queen is, and why she wants everyone on the Isle to expire. Whoever she is, I know how to get to her: Kemorte. I know that something is terribly off with him. Before we left the Isle, he was acting out of character. It wasn't until the confrontation between me and the crew that I felt like he wanted us to fail. I think he knew more than he led on, and I can only believe that it was because he is in league with the Dark Queen. I must stop him. I only hope that the whole prophecy is accurate, and we will suppress the darkness.

Keera

We sat in silence; each alone in our thoughts. Idava walked into the room, dressed in a flight suit that I've seen Raknico and his crew wear. "It still fits!" she exclaimed as she wrapped herself in a golden, hooded cape. "We have a lot to do and so little precious time." Raknico and I both looked at her like she had two heads. "You mean to come with us?" Raknico took the question right from my mind. "Well, yes. There is so much we must do to prepare, and time is of the essence. We must prepare Keera, Thena, and Mara for travel to the Isle. She can't just go as is, and she hasn't much time before the birth." I stood in shock. "What do you mean I don't have much time? I can't be more than a month or two, tops, pregnant. I have plenty of time." Raknico stepped in before Idava could speak. "She's right. It took about three Earth months to travel here with all my crew at high energy. Even with the extra people and energy powering the vessel, the team is not at full power so it will probably take longer. I don't think we will want to arrive too close to the birth. If we are, indeed, the chosen ones, we will bring a lot of attention to ourselves. I believe the people will automatically know. There will be a celebration. Then we will need to stand in front of the High Appointed on Mount Appointed."

"That's where I come in," Idava proclaimed. "I will help Raknico and his crew prepare the ship. I will also lead the acclimation process so that you and your sisters are not over-whelmed by the atmosphere on the Isle. Trust me, you will know the difference. This will take some time. You will also need a midwife. I learned a lot during my time here and so my knowledge will be very helpful when the time comes. People on the Isle do things a bit differently and your body will not be able to handle those methods. I am here for you and your sisters. I watched over you girls all these years and my job does not stop here." I took a deep breath and exhaled, "So, it's settled. We are all going back to the ship, then traveling to the Isle. I've never even been out of the state but will be adding space travel to my résumé." Idava waved me off, "Child, it is only space and time. You will be fine."

CHAPTER EIGHTEEN

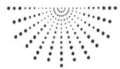

Raknico

*W*e teleport back into Keera's room. Idava told us she would meet us here once she finished with her errands... whatever that meant. It was morning now and the only thing I could think of is lying in bed with my mate, soothing her nerves to increase our collective strength. As we materialized in her room, I bent down to kiss her but was interrupted by someone who was already in the room. "Eh-hem. I hope you had a good trip." The voice belonged to Saniyah. Although I breathed a sigh of relief, I turned to face her and put myself between her and Keera. She was leaning on the desk, almost like she was patiently waiting for our return. "Oh, hi Saniyah. I didn't see you there. Umm... Keera and I were... she had something on her... I was trying a new questioning tech... nique."

Where are my thoughts.

"Oh, Nico, you already know that you don't need to go

around the truth with me. It's already known. I have to say that it amazes me that you've hidden it from me for this long." She closed her eyes and took a deep breath. "I mean you're mated!!!" Saniyah exclaimed, raising her voice slightly. She looked around, embarrassed, before continuing, "How?" Her eyes darted around. "This is unheard of." She turned her attention to Keera. "And you… There is still something different… I am drawn to you. What is it about you? I cannot pinpoint…" Raknico interrupted before she could dig deeper. "It's a rather hefty story, Nya. I need you to assemble everyone in the meeting room. We have a lot to do to prepare for our tr—" Saniyah's eyes were still on Keera, in a trance, trying to look deeper, when she remembered what she meant to say. "Kemorte is missing… along with an emergency ship." Keera looked at Saniyah in shock. I already knew it was just a matter of time before he slipped away. My being away must have been the perfect opportunity. "That's not all. Thena is also missing. I think he took her." At that revelation, Keera grabbed my hand and began to panic. "Why would he take her? Where is he going?" She looked so helpless. I sent her waves of good energy, but stopped when I noticed that she was already receiving calming energy. I was shocked. "He's healing you!" Forgetting that Saniyah was standing there, I reached down to rub Keera's belly. I spoke softly to it and thanked our son for already protecting my mate.

Saniyah took a step back and gasped. "She's pregnant, too?! I knew something was different, but I could have never imagined. How? There is too much going on right now that I need to know. Please, Nico." I reached out and touched Saniyah. She was skilled, so she extracted my memories, quickly processed them, then gasped again. "You two are the chosen? I always knew you were special, Raknico. I just never knew how special. I am pleased to be in your presence." She started to bow but I pulled her to her feet. "Saniyah. I need you to forget that for now and tell me: how long has your brother been gone?" She thought for a moment, "We all were weak from the negative emotions from the sisters. I don't know for sure. I found an energy projector in his suite. He may have been gone for a while. I haven't seen him in a long time... he could be anywhere... but where would he go?" He used an energy projector. A device that was invented by people of the Beneath. We still don't understand the reason behind the invention, but it allows the user to create energy in many forms, somewhat creating a diversion to confuse our kind into thinking a person is there when they are not. No matter for us, though, I knew where he was going. "Saniyah, please get everyone in the meeting room, including Mara. We need to prepare for our trip home. Make haste, because Kemorte has a head start."

CHAPTER NINETEEN

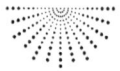

Keera

*I*dava arrived some time that afternoon with a handful of clothes and medical supplies. "Aunt Ida... I mean Idava, what is the purpose of the medical supplies. Won't Raknico be able to heal me if I need it?" There were so many supplies. *Did she rob a hospital?* No matter how she came across the supplies, I wanted to know their purpose. She continued to take inventory of her supplies. Without looking at me, she responded, "Child, we haven't had a natural-born child in centuries. What we have are 'spiritual births.'" I looked at her, stupefied. "Girl, do you know the story of Adam and Eve? How, because they ate of the fruit from the Tree of knowledge, women would have painful births?" I nod and she continues. "Well, you are still under the Adam and Eve Law, as I like to call it. Think of it this way: we have ascended above that decree. Because of the interference of the High Appointed, women no longer have pain while giving birth. The contractions are uncomfortable, but it's because it is stress energy. And as you know, negative energy is bad for our health. We combat that, not with drugs, but with positive energy. What you will experience… well, we don't have anything strong enough to combat it, so I need to bring whatever medicines I can to assist Raknico."

It made sense. It just upset me that I have to be in so much pain to give birth. The experience they have, what Idava expressed, sounded like a really enjoyable experience. But what I will experience seems like a fate worse than death. I left Idava to her work and started back to my room. I lay across the bed to rest for a moment. Since we'd been back I'd felt content. I first asked Saniyah to get me a pregnancy test. I believed them, but needed concrete proof to show Mara. It would be a lot for her to take in, so I needed something tangible to give her so that I could bring her back to reality. Mara was stubborn like that and the only way to reason with her was to give her evidence. I took the test and, of course, it was positive. Armed with the test, I went to see Mara. She looked worse for the wear. She was sad because she hadn't seen me or Thena in a while and thought that maybe something had happened to us. I had to give her the rundown and tell her about Thena. She cried for a while, and cried even harder when I told her that I would save her. I hoped that her tears were because she was happy that I was fighting for my family. Then, I commenced with telling her about me. Once I started telling her about Nico and I, she laughed hysterically. I think she was having trouble coping. When I pulled out the positive pregnancy test, I handed it to her. My hand grazed hers and shocked her with a burst of positive energy. She abruptly stopped laughing and looked down and saw the little blue plus sign. I'm sure she stopped breathing when she felt the energy buzz. She had so many questions that I just could not answer, but I left her with the comfort that Thena would be okay, and we would live to see another day after all this was over. She believed me right away, which was rare, and said that she would be by my side through it all.

I lifted myself from the bed, feeling uneasy. It seemed like the moment I was told I was pregnant… well, the moment I saw the positive test, I had been having pregnancy symptoms. I think my mind is playing tricks on me, because I've been getting nauseous so often that I have simply started eating crackers and drinking water all day, every day. Most of the time, the sight or smell of food turns me away. Idava said that it is possible the baby is so powerful that I am feeling the symptoms ten-fold. Whatever it is, I hope I don't suffer for the whole nine months. We will begin the acclimation process soon, so I have to get as much rest as I can. Grabbing the crackers from my desk, I lie back down and meditate on feeling better.

I must have drifted off because I was startled awake by my father's voice. I gasped and that's when I noticed that I was not alone. Raknico was there in the bed with me, and he displayed the same shock that I had so I know he heard it, too. We looked at each other, at a loss for words. Terafey's voice was as clear as if he was in the room. He said one word: "Hurry!"

Raknico

126

The next few weeks went by fast. After that joint illusion Keera and I had experienced, I moved our launch up. I know Keera and Mara needed to be acclimated, but we need to hurry so that no further damage can be done by Kemorte and the Dark Queen. Time is definitely of the essence. Keera has been sick these last weeks and she has begun to reveal her pregnancy. The acclimation has been hard on her, but the baby has been healing her just right. I never knew that our atmosphere would be harmful to humans, since their atmosphere is not harmful to us. Idava said that both atmospheres are almost identical, with the only difference being that my atmosphere is spiritually stronger and more electrically charged than Keera's. It hurts so much to see her scream or shake from the pressure but in each session, she gets stronger and stronger, so now she just winces when the session starts. Next, she will be learning how to speak in our atmosphere. Most of our people will not understand her, but the practice will still be good for preparation. We leave tonight at midnight. I am eager to get home, to battle this great evil, and welcome my baby into this world. I have been communicating with the baby... well, trying to, at least. It's strange because whenever I hear the baby's voice, it's like the baby is in a tunnel and the voice echoes. I've asked Idava about this, trying to see if there is a defect in the child because of the difference in mother and father, and all she has to say is, 'All is well... try not to worry about things that are beyond your control.' I should be able to hear the baby loud and clear, not like he's a mile away in a tunnel, but I take her answer as a good thing. I trust that she would tell me if something was wrong.

Keera

I really do miss the days when life was simpler. It seems like Idava does not know the meaning of the word rest. I try to tell her that I am far too sick for her lessons and she tells me 'a little nausea never killed anyone.' She says that as long as I am eating and keeping it down, which I am, I can keep moving forward. The lessons are getting easier. I remember my reaction to the first lesson. The level of energy that hit me was so fierce that it vibrated throughout my whole body. It was like an invasion and, in feeling that, I fought it off. I vaguely remembered Idava telling me not to fight, but it was almost like an immune-response; I had to save myself from the invasion. After that lesson, I was chastised about fighting, being reminded that the first lesson was not the full effect of the Isle. Working with the energy, instead of against, was the key to surviving. For each lesson after that, I tried to remember not to fight and move with the energy. It was diffi-cult at first, and I was still screaming and shaking to deflect the energy but once I got the hang of it, I actually enjoyed the feeling. When Mara gained enough strength, Idava brought us together to learn how to interact in that high energy. For the first time, Mara was able to get into my mind and speak to me, and she loved it. Eventually she was able to communicate with the baby, too, which made her feel like a proud aunt. Every-thing was progressing as it should, except I was worried about the baby. Everyone, including myself, says the baby sounds far away; that communicating with the baby is not like they've experienced before. Saniyah tells me that it should be like talking to someone standing right in front of you. not like there are miles between. Idava assures me that, although what we are experiencing is rare, there is nothing to worry about. Nico and I share our fears, but comfort each other, knowing that we are doing what we were meant to be doing. I am showing now, so I know the baby is growing. I feel its strength and it's almost unbearable, so I know it's growing strong. We leave tonight and I pray to whoever is listening that we succeed.

CHAPTER TWENTY

*E*veryone was set and ready to go. They met in the hibernation chamber, where Raknico briefed everyone on the procedures for flying. The room was aglow with the humming of energy. There were lights and buttons all over the walls, and the center of the room was configured circularly, with hibernation containers used to extract energy from the flyers. Each person was assigned a container so that they could be monitored. Keera was placed in the middle of Raknico and Idava, in case anything went wrong with the pregnancy. The hibernation containers were made to suspend the life force of a person, so that eating and drinking was not necessary for travel. This was the first time an unborn child traveled, so Idava volunteered to watch over all beings traveling. Her container would allow her to carry on with normal life, while extracting her energy. She would use it mostly as a sleeping chamber. Helping Keera into her container, Idava reassured her that she wouldn't even realize that time had passed. She would go to sleep and wake up feeling like she had just lain down. The only indicator of time passing would be the control panel showing time elapsed, and the size of her growing belly. Keera smiled with excitement; thinking about what it would be like to wake up larger and filled with more life! On one hand, she was sad that she would miss moments with the baby, but on the other hand she was thankful for the rest. Mara hugged Keera, teary eyed, giving her goodbyes. Keera sent a wave of calm to her, letting her know that it was only see you later. Once everyone retreated to their containers, the launch began. The slight buzz of the ship started to grow into a louder hum. The sound began to lull everyone to sleep. The energy from each container flowed through tubes leading to the mainframe of the ship. Once everyone was suspended, the ship rose and blasted off into the distance, leaving no trace that it had been there for many months.

PART III
THE ISLE OF VAEHTE

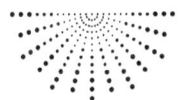

CHAPTER TWENTY-ONE

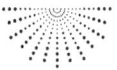

Keera

I began to rouse. It felt like there were a million voices attacking my brain. There were so many electrical impulses vibrating throughout my body. My mind screamed for help but I heard Idava's voice say, *'Don't fight... let it flow through you.'* I slowly began to relax and focus on the electricity. It flowed through me and surprisingly made me feel free, energized, and like I could take on the world. I slowly opened my eyes. Above me, Idava and Raknico were staring at me. I began to come into awareness of my surroundings. Among the electricity, I could hear my sister Mara screaming. I shot up, looking around. Idava grabbed me at the shoulders. "Slow down, child. You don't want to hurt yourself." My eyes saw Mara's distress. She was screaming, with her hands over her ears, while Shanluk tried calming her. He was speaking to her in calming tones in his native tongue. She looked at him intensely and eventually heard his words.

Slowly, her breathing calmed. Shanluk cupped his hands on top of Mara's, resting over her ears. They looked at each other with so much passion it was hard to tear my eyes away. I would have never guessed the renegade would have such a soft heart.

After staring for what felt like minutes, I felt as if I was eavesdropping on a special moment. So, I brought my attention back to Idava and Raknico. Idava was using her fingers to check my heart rate on my wrist. Raknico took his time to inspect me. He inspected each part of my body and used our connection to make sure I was still sound of mind. I wasn't sure how long we were asleep because it really felt like I had just closed my eyes. Like my body had finally relaxed but unceremoniously got jerked back to reality. Raknico's focus remained on my midsection. I could feel his excitement. I brought my eyes to my belly and saw that there was, indeed, something to look at. I was wearing a big tee-shirt, but you could see the growing baby beneath my shirt. I gasped. I touched my belly and felt my baby move. It was incredible! I couldn't contain myself. "Nico, feel here. The baby is moving!" Raknico put his hand on my stomach and closed his eyes. He smiled. "He is really strong. Just like his mother." Returning the smile, I put my hand on top of Raknico's, making the connection complete. I turned to Idava, "I'm bigger than I thought I would be." I looked down at my stomach. "Idava, are we okay?" Idava looked between us. "Child, every woman is different. But you must remember: what's in here," she touched my belly, causing the baby to respond, "is special. Don't worry. I would alert you if there was something wrong."

She smiled at me and squeezed my hand. She left to tend to Mara.

Raknico stood by my side, beaming with excitement. It was a very weird feeling. I could feel the thoughts and energy from those on the planet, but I felt Raknico deep in my bones, as if they were my own. Placing his hands above my own, Raknico closed his eyes and began to sense the baby. "He is very strong. The new environment is like second nature. No adjustments are necessary! Amazing!" He smiled so wide that I couldn't help but be excited about our new journey. Raknico knelt down to kiss me. Our foreheads touched and I was instantly electrified and filled with soothing calm waves. He helped me to my feet. I was amazed that I didn't fall over because my stomach was so big. I gave my body a good stretch. I thought I would be terribly stiff and uncomfortable, but my body felt like it had been given a spa week and didn't even realize that there was a baby growing in there, taking space away from my necessary organs. I looked around the room. Everyone was still waking up and, of course, my sister and I were still adjusting to the new environment. After Mara stopped screaming and looking like a balloon ready to pop, Shanluk guided her toward the door. We were about to exit the craft and be greeted by the Vaehte people.

Raknico said that although the Vaehte people speak tele-pathically, to me and my sisters, it would feel like they were all speaking out loud. I imagined a public event, like a football game, and that is exactly how it felt. Raknico had given me a crash course on some of their customs. They bow when they greet. If you are a familiar, which is a person who is an associate, friend, or family member, there is a type of handshake, which is their only form of physical contact, that is performed where each person grabs the forearm of the person they are greeting and they exchange a moment of positive energy. It was strange, because I felt like they were no different from us on Earth. I know I have seen people shake hands by grasping forearms, bring it in for a hug, and exchange pleasantries. I believe that verbal pleasantries can turn into positive energy; well, at least make you have a more positive outlook on the moment or day. We reached the outer-lock door. This was the final step before being immersed into a foreign place. I paused. Sensing my hesitation, Raknico stopped and faced me. "You know, you can stay behind and wait a while. There's no rush... well, there is, but I doubt a few moments will matter." I looked up and smiled appreciatively, "Nico, I'm ready, just a bit nervous. We have a job to do and as long as you are there by my side, I'll be fine." Raknico led me through the door. Before the door fully opened, my body was humming with the conversations of everyone out there. Once the door was opened, it almost felt like I got my mind to myself once again. What I saw was beyond what I could possibly describe or imagine. I moved forward and grabbed Mara's hand. She looked at me and then back at the scene in front of us. There were millions of people around the ship, waiting to greet us. Not a single thought was being conveyed because of the anticipation of receiving news from the mission. The sky, if that's what you could call it, was filled with so many stars, and the moon. They looked so close, like I could reach up and grab them. It was night, according to the time, but there was an abundance of moonlight, making it appear to be earlier than it was. The moon appeared to be looming, resting on the horizon, illuminating our surroundings. I looked around, taking it all in, and saw the landscape. Everything was in full blossom. It was so green and just beautiful. There were rolling hills, and flowers of every color imaginable. The air was warm, like the sun was still high in the sky, and smelled of roses and lavender. It wasn't like a smothering summer day. It was more like a comfortable, overcast, spring day on the beach. I couldn't help but imagine myself at the beach, enjoying the most perfect day.

I was pulled out of my admiration of the land when I noticed Idava's arms moving around in conversational gestures. I had no clue what was happening. I felt like I was being left out of the conversation when I began to feel a nagging behind my ears. I gave into the sensation, and then was able to hear Idava. I felt some collective surprise and anxiety that was quickly alleviated. It was amazing to see how the balance was restored so quickly. I didn't understand what she was saying, but it sound very inspirational and important. She gestured back to Raknico and I. Raknico began to walk forward, from behind Idava, while reassuring me. I followed him and soon we were in front, and out in the open. There was a collective gasp from the crowd, and the murmurs in my mind started again. I looked back at Mara, to make sure she was okay, but saw that Shanluk was already there, soothing her. Those two looked cute together. I need to remember to ask Mara about that later. I turned back and saw that the people were very excited. They were mentally hooting and simply beaming with positive energy. Raknico was looking at me, smiling. "What!?" I had no clue what was going on. He bent down to whisper, "You are sharing your thoughts." I instantly turned bright red and turned away. "Oh gosh! I have to watch it. Did everyone hear me?" Raknico was chuckling to himself, "Yes, but only those who understand your language know what you said." Satisfied with that answer, I turned to look at Mara and saw she was blushing slightly. I sent her a mental sorry and she smiled an okay. I turned back to face the crowd, who were still very excited.

"Wait, if no one understood me, why are they all so excited?"

"They are excited that the prophecy is coming to pass. Also, someone revealed that your presence has already improved conditions here." Raknico's face saddened a little. It wasn't too noticeable, but because I could feel his emotions, I knew something was wrong. "Why are you sad? I thought that was part of my job." He grabbed my hands and kissed them. "It is your job. I just fear that, because you are already being sensed so strongly, the people here aren't the only ones who can sense your arrival." I smiled, but I knew who he meant. We didn't have much time before we were going to have to face the Dark Queen and Kemorte.

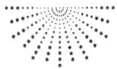

CHAPTER TWENTY-TWO

Keera

The celebration was nothing like what I expected. There was a lot of music and dancing but it was nothing like what we had back home. The music pulsed through your body and soul. There was no sound to it; only pulsations evoking a feeling within. It filled me with such great energy that I had no choice but to be happy. Raknico told Mara and I that the music was similar to ours, as in it evoked a state of being in each person differently, depending on how they interpreted the song. I couldn't hear, let alone understand, the lyrics but we were assured that eventually telepathy would become second nature to us.

We were seated at the grand table. The big chair at the end was left empty. I assumed it was the Grand Father's chair, but said nothing because I didn't want to bring anyone down. "Yes, the chair belongs to my father." I turned around to see that Raknico had returned to the table with our drinks, and had also heard what I was thinking. "My first lesson needs to be on how to guard my thoughts." I thought that I was fairly skilled, but this was a whole other level of skill to acquire. Taking the seat next to me, Raknico grabbed my hand and gave it a squeeze, "My sweet mate, there is nothing you can guard from me. I hear everything, and if I don't hear it, I will sense it." He smiled at me so deviously. I returned the smile, knowing I would not want anything different between us. His face then became serious. "But I agree that we need to teach you how to guard your thoughts. Most beings will not understand your words, but may piece it together based on your emotions. We need to be on guard at all times, in case Kemorte shows his face." I nodded.

Feeling a little helpless and out of place, I begin to pick at my food with my head down, making sure not to look at anyone or think any thoughts, which was proving to be very difficult. Mara's laughs caught me off guard. I looked up and saw her dancing with Shanluk. She looked amazing, like she belonged here, with him. I couldn't help but smile. She looked happy and that, in turn, made me happy. It was short-lived when I began to think about Thena. Well, it was not exactly my thinking about Thena, but more like I heard a cry of help from Thena. *She's here!* I stood up, looking to every face in attendance to see if Thena was in the crowd. I focused a little more. She was not in the room, but she felt near. I knew I couldn't see her. My head was pounding due to her loud cries mixing in with the music and the people around me. I lost focus. I had to bring my hands to my head as I tried to use my hands as a buffer between the sounds. I must have looked like I was in terrible pain because before I knew it, the pulsation from the music stopped and Shanluk, Mara, Idava, Saniyah, and Raknico were by my side. I blocked out all their concerns and tried to focus on Thena's voice. It was then that I felt it for certain. She was not at the party, but Kemorte was. He was standing so far back that I could barely see him but through every fiber of my being, I felt him and knew it was him. He was transmitting what I could only think of as ransom footage, to me. Everyone around me could sense my fear and anxiety, but could not understand what was causing the damaging change in emotion. Raknico was the only eyewitness to my torment. He was the one who could neutralize my pain. Once I spotted Kemorte, he sent an even stronger vision toward me that knocked me off balance. Thena was in a dark place. It was a place where life ceased to exist. She was holding her ears and screaming. It reminded me of when Mara first arrived here. As fast as the vision came, Kemorte removed it and sent a verbal message. "Meet me there at nightfall. Don't worry if you don't know your way, your *mate* can tell you where it is," he said the word 'mate' with so much hatred, it made my skin crawl. Kemorte continued, "Once he shows you the entrance, you must come in alone. If not, you will never see your sister, alive, again." Once the message was received and processed, I was able to breathe again. It was then that I noticed that I was being held up by Nico. I struggled to find my own footing. Once up, I found that I was moved to a more private area where only Raknico, Mara, Saniyah, and Idava were standing around. Shanluk and another warrior were running back, "We lost him. I don't know how he managed to move so fast, and without leaving an energy trail, but he's gone."

"I don't think he was here... I mean actually, physically here." Everyone looked at me, puzzled. "What do you mean, child?" It was Idava's turn to be in the dark, wondering what was transpiring. I looked at her, then to the rest of the group, "He... I believe he has mastered the art of astral-projection, or something similar. Whatever it is, he was able to appear, and make my sister appear, in my mind. Nico saw it. It was so surreal." Nico simply nodded. "He wants me to bring Keera to The Beneath. I think he wants to exchange Thena for Keera." There was a collective mental gasp around the room. "I can't do it!" I turned my head and stared in shock at what Raknico had said. He grabbed my hands and held them tight, "I can't let him have you or our child. We will figure out another way." He placed a hand on my swollen belly. As he did this, the baby sent a burst of energy.

The energy gave me new resolve. "No!" I said, giving everyone a strong mental shock. "We are going to do this. My sister is important to me and I will not allow her to stay in Kemorte's hands any longer than she has to be." I took a deep breath and guided Nico into a more private area of the room. "Look, I know you're scared. I am, too, but I am not going to let him get away with this. He is trying to bully us and I will not let it happen. Please, you have to trust me. We will win." I brought my hand up to cup his face. He covered my hand with his own. "We will do this and win." He nodded and kissed the palms of my hands, taking time on each palm to savor the moment. Our energy began to swirl and send blasts out to all around, filling the Isle with appreciative energy.

CHAPTER TWENTY-THREE

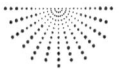

Raknico

I never thought that I would be in a position where I would have to send my mate to the slaughterhouse. There isn't even a small piece of me that trusts Kemorte. I know he is up to something sinister, and the Queen of the Beneath is pulling all the strings. Kemorte has never been a strong being. Well, physically he looks able, but mentally, his will was easily bent. He always needed someone to pull him along; never a leader, always a follower. I have always felt bad for my cousin, but not anymore. From the moment Keera received the visions from Kemorte, I've had to mask my true feelings. I feel like I want to rip Kemorte apart for everything he is doing wrong; for the stress alone. But at the same time, I need to be supportive of Keera and her abilities. I know she is strong, and I know that she will be able to survive anything. I just don't want to take any chances. My child's life is being challenged, and I seem to be the only one who is trying to protect it. I try not to think about it because I know that Keera would never let anything happen to our child. I also try to put faith in Idava, because I know she would tell me if I had anything to worry about. Either way, it wouldn't matter; I would worry anyway. I've begun to have very strong human emotions and if I am not careful, I will be headed to the beneath myself. *No*. I vow to never be like Kemorte. *Never!* After Keera and I spoke in private, and I gave her my nod of support and approval, we returned to the group to create a plan. The key to the instructions from Kemorte was Keera needed to be alone. He has to know on some level that I would never allow that to happen. In that case, he must be expecting me, and if so, I need to figure out how to get one step ahead of him.

Keera was surprisingly much more positive and strong on my planet. It almost seems as though, by being here, she has come to the place where she was always meant to be. It was almost as if she was from my world, but got lost somehow. As we made our way to one of the many gateways to the Beneath, I could feel Keera's trepidation. I grabbed her hand and gave it a squeeze so that she knew she was not alone. The plan was to have our small recovery group track our movements. but not follow us through. Idava was very strong and talented and had the ability to track our child. I would walk in with Keera and once we were close to the meeting place, I was going to hang back, watch from afar, while Keera altered the energy to mask my location. She is very talented and I knew that just by being on my planet, she would have the strength to showcase some of those talents. I pulled Keera to a stop. We had reached our separation point and I wanted to kiss her before all the drama. "Keera, I want you to know that I have full trust in you. But if anything goes wrong, you can reach out to me mentally and I will come to you." Her hands were shaking within mine. She slowly looked up to me, "I know. I love you." She pulled her hands from my grasp. I brought my hands to her belly, brought my face down, and kissed her belly. I stood and sent Keera a burst of encouragement before she turned and walked away. I watched her as her figure became smaller and smaller, the further away she became. I continued to watch, unable to tear my gaze away. After standing motionless for what felt like an eternity, I began to make my way to the place where I was to stay until Keera summoned me. We decided that I should remain close to the entrance of the Beneath, behind my strongest mental wall, to avoid detection. There was an over-grown area of trees and brush that looked perfect for blending in. When I arrived, I took a moment to meditate, to connect with the greenery, and prepare my mental block. After feeling mentally fortified, my mind automatically began to run through our last moments, building a perfect image of Keera in my mind. The simple thought of her brought so much joy to my being. The image turned to the nervous Keera that left me watching her walk away. I was filled with trepidation. *I shouldn't have let her go.* I began to pace, feeling the energy surge, causing pressure to build behind my eyes. I turned to leave the safety of the trees, focused on locating Keera. As I prepared myself to enter the Beneath, I felt something sting the back of my head, causing me to drop to my knees. I pressed my fingers to the wound, to try and understand what had happened. Pulling my hands back revealed a wet, sticky substance. *Blood.* I looked around, trying to figure out what had hit me, or what I had walked into, but found that my eyes were losing focus. I tried to stand but found that my balance was off, as well. I stayed on my hands and knees, fighting the nausea I felt. I closed my eyes and tried to get a read on the energy around me. The darkness deepened and my body felt as if I were being drained. I dropped to my forearms, then to the fetal position, on the ground. I laid there, hyperventilating, as I felt the life drain out of me. With my last drop of consciousness, I thought of Keera.

Keera

My legs trembled as I walked toward the direction leading to Kemorte. With each step, my heartbeat drummed through my ears, creating an uneven sound disturbance in the otherwise silent surroundings. My interactions with Kemorte were minimal and, at that thought, I slowed my walk down almost to a halt. I grasped at the closest structure when I felt my pulse quicken and breathing become uneasy. Sweat pooled in the creases on my body as my body temperature rose and vision blurred. *Get it together Kee.* I put an arm around my belly and accepted the baby's loving energy, which settled my nerves and cooled my skin. *Nico.* New resolve filled my mind as I thought about Raknico, and why I am meeting with Kemorte and endangering my child. *I won't let anything happen to you. I promise.* I stood up straight and pressed on. I wasn't sure what Kemorte was capable of, nor was I comfortable with the fact that it wasn't a level playing field, but I would win. I had to. He may have the upper-hand-- and my sister, but he doesn't know what I am capable of. I pushed the thoughts of being led to slaughter away and thought, instead, of the reasons for putting myself in danger. *My baby. Thena. The Isle.* I kept moving forward without looking back, reminding myself that Thena's safety, and the safety of the Isle, was at stake. As if a lightbulb illuminated the darkness attempting to invade my soul, I determined that I would live and I would fulfill the prophecy. My sister needed me; Raknico needed me; My baby needed me; my people, too.

As I walked down what looked to be a four-lane road, I couldn't shake the feeling of familiarity. My view of the world was limited to my small town and television, but for reasons I couldn't grasp, recognition was skirting the edges of my mind. *What is this place?* I shrugged it off, as I needed a clear mind to prepare for what lie ahead. I took a few deep breaths, thinking only of the purity I felt when I first arrived at the Isle. Instinctually, my thoughts returned to Raknico. Our love created the bridge between our worlds, and the life growing inside me. There was nothing more pure. I sent Raknico a thought and a burst of love. My breath hitched. I had been so lost in my thoughts that I didn't even notice Raknico's absence in my mind. He felt like he was sleeping, dreamlessly. *Why would he be sleeping, or feel like he is sleeping, at a moment like this?*

I stopped walking and reached out again, more urgently. *Where are you?* I tried and could not get a read on Raknico. I began to hyperventilate as fear racked my body. My vision turned red and I felt angry for not being able to reach him. This place was affecting me, and with fear crawling up from the ground, trying to pull me under, I felt that Nico needed me.

I made one more attempt to find Raknico in my mind. When I didn't find him in any corner, I lost my strength to move forward. I cursed my cowardice and myself, for feeling like I was nothing without his support. I rubbed my belly in defeat. "I can't be someone's mother," I whispered, as if saying it aloud added value. *I can't even rescue my sister.* The tears fell easily, creating droplets down the front of my shirt. I cried until pain gathered at my forehead. I grabbed the nearest structure, audibly exhaling, attempting to stop myself from crying. Exhaustion began to take over and suddenly I felt faint. As I looked around for a place to sit, I felt joy erupting from inside my womb. The love emanated from deep within and, without words, I knew I was loved. The anger and sadness began to ebb, being replaced by determination and strength. Memories of Thena flooded my mind, followed by some with Raknico. I caught a few glimpses of me, holding something illuminated in my arms and, instinctively, I knew it was my baby. My baby. *How are you doing this?* At that moment, I knew this had to be done. Fear or not, I had too many people counting on me. I straightened my back, sending energy to my baby, thanking him or her for reviving me. I took a step and something zapped me, causing me to fall to my hands and knees. Panting, I turned my head to the side, trying to get a glimpse of what was there. I looked back and saw two figures approaching me. *Did they tase me?* "I see someone has been busy." I turned my head to the other side, trying to see the other figure slowly walking toward me. "I heard about how you people reproduce." My hair was in my face and all that I saw was their head, shaking in disgust. "Get her up." I was yanked up by my armpits by the first two figures. I felt faint and everything was going dark around me. "Let's move, we have a lot of work to do before we present them to the Queen."

It finally clicked. I knew that voice. *Kemorte*. He had planned this all along. I was willingly coming to him, and it still wasn't enough. Panic seized me as I struggled against the arms that held me up. My feet failed me and I no longer had any coordination. I wanted to yell 'stop', but I had lost the ability to use my voice. My legs buckled and my captors continued walking, dragging my feet along. My heartbeat quickened as I felt my consciousness wane. Fear crept up, yet again, as I thought about my current predicament. Before the darkness claimed me, the words Kemorte said came rushing back-- *Them*, he said, 'Them'.

I woke up lying on my side on the floor. I kept my eyes shut so that I could listen to things around me and reach out to the baby to make sure it was still ok. The baby was fine. Nothing had been done to my child, so I sighed in relief. I felt Raknico nearby. His presence was dampened, but near nonetheless. I slowly opened my eyes. I was lying on a marble floor. It must have been a great hall in its day. The building was in ruins but the floors were still in good shape. My hands were tied behind my back, but not with rope. I tried to move to get an idea of where I was, and with whom, but had trouble due to my expanding stomach. After a few attempts while grunting, I heard footsteps approaching. I tried to steady my heart but had so much anxiety that there was no way I could play possum. The footsteps drew nearer and stopped. "Ahh, so she's awake. I was wondering when you were gonna grace us with your presence." It was Kemorte, so I panicked. I began to struggle against my invisible binds. "Expected rope? It's energy ribbon... I control it, so you can't break it. Pretty neat, huh?!" I rolled my eyes in his general direction. "Can you please at least sit me up?" Kemorte pondered this for a second before signaling to his minions to lift me onto a chair. "I don't think sitting would hurt anything." I surveyed the room. In the corner, I saw Raknico sitting on the floor, tied up as I am with what I can only think of as a forcefield. "Nico!" I rose and tried to run to him. I was stopped by an invisible barrier that gave me a shock when I ran into it. "He can't hear you. Nor can you hear him. You can't communicate mentally, either! All you can do is look at each other from across the room and wish to be together." He laughed like a lunatic. "I just love it!"

I sat back in the chair. He was here the whole time, behind me, and I hadn't even known. There had to be a flaw in this. We can't just be captured and lose, just like that. I closed my eyes to focus. "It won't work. Trust me." I ignored Kemorte and continued to focus. I remembered when I had caused my father to fall to his knees from my mental calls. From a small corner of my mind, I could hear Nico. It wasn't clear, but I needed him to know I heard him. As loud as I could get my mind, I yelled to Nico, *I hear you. When I open my eyes, nod to let me know you heard me.* I opened my eyes and searched Raknico's face. His eyes were wide and he gave a small nod. I rejoiced inside, but turned my attention back to Kemorte, who was still talking.

"... you just wait until you meet my Queen. You will give in to her, or you will never see your sister again!" Just as he finished talking, I saw movement in my peripheral vision. My eyes darted to Raknico because his eyes were wide and his face was white with shock. I turned to see the object of his shock. It was his... mother, Nima. Kemorte bowed to the ground. "My Queen." It was now my turn to be shocked. From what I had gathered from Raknico's memories and father's stories, Nima disappeared while Nico was still young. She looked the way I'd seen her in their memories, just slightly different, probably due to the energy differences between the Isle and the Beneath. "Raknico, son, it's been so long." I guess she felt the need to help us recover from the shock. "You are wondering how I became the queen. It's a dreadfully long story." I began to shoot questions her way, filling in the space of my invisible jail cell. She raised her hand in the air to halt speech. "Kemorte, do lower the barriers. I can only hear one person at a time."

"As you wish, my Queen." I guess we were both asking questions and her highness couldn't handle it. When the barrier lowered, I could once again feel whole with Raknico. I looked at him and gave him my most sincere and sympathetic expression. I couldn't imagine what this must be like for him. "Well, son, you wanted to know why I abandoned you. While your mate here," speaking as if the word "mate" was sour in her mouth, "-- doesn't care how long the story is, as long as I tell it." She approached me and grabbed me forcefully by my chin. "Let's get one thing straight. I don't take orders from anyone. You will respect me, or this will end a lot sooner than I had planned." She tossed me back and I slumped in the seat, without another comment. Nico probed me to make sure we were uninjured. I tried to reassure him, but all I could feel was his anger building up. I tried to send calmness. We needed to stay level-headed.

Nima continued, "Where was I? Oh, yes... you see, I am the preceding oracle's daughter. I know, I know, the High Appointed are not to conceive when appointed. I was actually born before my mother was appointed. She was simply an average seer. Nothing special. I think it was me who gave her the power to become something great, but she never acknowledged it. Regardless, mother became the first High Appointed in history to have a family." Taking advantage of her moment to feel full of herself, I sent Raknico a mental message to keep attention away from me, at all costs, because I had a plan. "Everyone believed my father died before I was born. Ha ha! My father fell from grace and my mother was too ashamed, so she lied about it to everyone... Even to the preceding Grand Father." I began to gather my strength within my mind. I tried not to call on any extra energy, so as not to disturb the flow in the atmosphere, that would bring attention to myself. "I was the only child within the High Appointed walls. I was lonely. My mother had her duties and I was left alone to my own devices. Most days I would spend my time running around or reading books. Then, one night, I had a dream. The man in my dream told me he was my father, and that he wasn't dead. I was happy! I wanted a father, someone who wasn't looking for perfection. He said that if I wanted to find him, all I had to do was look into the looking glass and we could see each other. So that's what I did, I went to the looking glass and there he was. The man that was my father was extraordinary! He loved living in the Beneath! There was much more usable energy. He began to teach me things and my mother began to take notice. She caught me one day. She told me to never trust him. He was wrong in his ideas and that one day his kind would be recycled, and once again all would be perfect again. I DIDN'T WANT PERFECT!! I wanted what my father had."

She was silent for a moment, lost in her thoughts. I had almost unlocked myself from the binds. I told Raknico to encourage her. He asked, "So, what happened? What did you do?" She broke from her trance and continued, "Well, my father taught me things for years. One day, when I was old enough, I traveled to the Beneath and met him face to face. We came up with a plan. He told me that the only way to prevent perfection was to stop the prophecy from coming to pass. So, here we are." The bonds finally came undone. I sent a mental note to Raknico that I was free. "What about me? Did I mean anything to you, *Mother*?" The last word was like spitting poison. She looked longingly at him. "Raknico, I did care about you and your father at one point, but I had a mission to carry out and I had to eliminate all obstacles." She moved further into the room and now I was situated behind her. The bonds were gone, so I proceeded to move toward the door. My plan was flawed. I didn't know what I was going to do if, and when, I found an exit but I planned to find some help, then rescue Raknico and Thena before it was too late.

Raknico

I watched as Keera slowly crawled away, while my mother continued toward me. I hoped she had a good plan, because with all this talk of elimination, I didn't think Nima planned to have me around for long. She knelt down. "I have to say,

Terafey was very clever with keeping you a secret. If I'd known you were part of the prophecy, I would have gotten rid of you as a boy and we wouldn't even be here right now." Sadness enveloped me, but quickly dissipated when I thought of my own child. "Where is my father, anyway?" I bit out. She stood up and looked down on me. Her facial expression was of curiosity but quickly became unfeeling. "He and that human whore are here. But you will never find them. I want him to rot and starve to death for keeping you a secret from me." My mother grabbed me by my shirt and began to pull me up. This was it. I was never going to see my child, or see the world, become something better.

"Look what I found wandering the halls!" I looked up at the sound of Kemorte's voice to see he had Keera in his arms, with his hand over her mouth. She was trying to fight and get away, and at the same time, keep the baby safe. My mother focused on Keera. "Well, well. Clever girl. Just hold on to her. I want Raknico to watch me end her, and that bastard she carries." She tossed me to the side and instantly, I was behind another barrier. I was powerless. How was I to protect my family? I looked away because I was disgusted with myself. My mother stalked toward Keera. The room began to charge and buzz all around us. Nima seemed to not notice the change in the energy. As she got closer, it was like time stood still. Nima was moving very slowly toward Kemorte and Keera, and the room was overflowing with that pure energy that could only come from Keera and our baby. Just then, I had an epiphany. I looked at Keera, who was fighting for her life. I spoke mentally as loud as I could in order to breach the barrier: *You can absorb or deflect. You can absorb, or deflect.* Her eyes went wide and she went slack in his arms. I instantly thought something was wrong, but powerless as I was, I had to trust that Keera had a plan.

Keera

The conversation came back to me: *You can absorb it or deflect it. You need to understand both. It may save your life one day.* I now understood. I needed to survive and I had to defeat those who tried to stop me. I reached out to the baby and it was like he was already onboard with the plan. I took a deep breath and began to draw energy from those around me, into myself. Since Kemorte was touching me, his energy was absorbed fairly quickly. He drew a knife but because I was taking his energy, it felt as if I was the one drawing the knife. I pulled his energy faster, causing him to drop the knife, and then he dropped right behind me. I didn't check to ensure he was still alive. I left him with a small amount of energy to keep him alive long enough to see his fate. The energy was buzzing around inside me and it was becoming too much to bear. Without warning, Nima rushed me and her hands found their way around my neck. "How could you!? You are destroying everything I've worked for and you will pay!" She was cutting off my air supply, and fast. I felt myself fading and, without thinking, I released all the extra energy within myself and it carried her away like a strong gust of wind. I dropped to my knees, feeling exhausted. I cupped one arm around my belly and I felt that the baby was okay. I heard Nico yelling in the distance. It took almost the last bit of strength I had to rise up. He was still sitting under the forcefield, it was weak but still effective. How was this possible? Kemorte was neutralized.

"Nima, this doesn't have to be the end. Mother!!" I looked at Nico, who was yelling at the broken wall. He turned to me, "She's hanging there. I know it. We need to stop her from falling." I didn't respond. I felt the pain that he was feeling over his mother. No matter the situation, he just wanted love from his mother, like all children. I released Nico from the barrier. He ran and gathered me in his arms and we walked over to the ledge. As he had said, Nima was hanging and nearly falling off the edge. As we approached, she looked up, struggling to hold on. "Raknico, I wish things could have been different, I do. I wish your father would have seen things differently and life would have been so different for you. But I knew you would never see things my way. That's why I had to leave, and I'm sorry for that." He looked at me to ensure that I could stand. I nodded before he spoke again. "Please... Please Mother... We can make it work. What's wrong with that?" Raknico knelt down and held out his hand. Nima looked at it, "I'd rather die than live in the world that you and your mate are about to create." Raknico looked at her with pleading in his eyes, "Where's my father? Take my hand and we can be a family together. Again." A small tear streamed down her cheek. "I can't." She gave him a lingering look, and you could see that there was no changing her mind. "I am not perfect. I could never live in your world." She gave him one last look, and that's when I saw it. She was never told she was enough and, therefore, didn't believe that she could ever be more than what she is. I started to speak as Nima let go of the ledge and fell at least thirty feet. After the dust settled, we could see her, lying there, staring up at us. Nico sat down and mourned for his mother for a second time. It was hard for me to understand why he felt he could change her, but I did understand his desire to try. She, herself, didn't think she could change. I simply held him in my arms while he cried and mourned the life he would have had, if his mother would have stayed.

CHAPTER TWENTY-FOUR

Keera

*N*ico and I stayed locked in each other's arms for a long time. It had been awhile since he stopped crying, but I waited for him to show signs of being ready to move. I didn't want to rush him, yet I was eager to get to Thena. When I crawled away during Nima's monologue, I was able to get down the hall and to a stairwell. I could feel Thena down there. I moved swiftly down the stairs and saw that Thena was locked away in a cell, blocked by an energy barrier. She was also tied up with that energy ribbon Kemorte had engineered. I was able to unlock her energy ribbon, but before I could work on the barrier, Kemorte grabbed me and took me away from Thena. I fought as hard as I could, but it was like I was weakened by some unknown force. Kemorte was groping me, getting a good feel all over my body. I felt most violated when he touched my stomach, causing the baby to react. "Wait until my Queen sees that I recaptured you. She will allow me to kill you myself. Such a shame; there is so much I could have done with you... if it wasn't for my kin. He always had to have it all!" I let him talk so that I could distract him. "I wanted you to myself! But he had to be the one to question you. He always had to be in charge. You had no opportunity to fall in love with me!" Each time his grip loosened, I tried to get free and he would tighten his grip on me. "You would have been mated to me, and carrying my child." He didn't understand how his own traditions worked, but kept ranting on, "I heard stories about the traditional way of mating and before I kill you, I shall experience it for myself." Before I knew it, we were back in the room where Nico and Nima were still face-to-face. I winced at the memory. I tried not to relive the past, I knew I had to stay in the present and comfort Raknico. I just held him close, thankful that we had lived through our hellish ordeal.

Raknico

I sat, lost in my thoughts. I couldn't believe it! My mother was alive all these years and didn't once see how I was doing, or care to know what I had been up to. She took her own life, in front of my own eyes, because she didn't want to be in the world that I was bringing forth. She didn't want to be in my life; she didn't want me, her own son. It hurt to the core, but the anger I felt toward her was more than the sadness I felt from losing my mother a second time. These negative emotions were consuming me, and I let them. She took my father away from me; Keera's mother away. She was going to kill me and my family to fulfill her selfish desires. She was not even curious about the world that would come to pass through Keera and me. I felt a jolt from Keera. I looked over at her and she was just running her arm across my back. It was gentle, but a strong reminder that I needed to stay within the confines of our energy and let go of the Beneath. I closed my eyes and focused. Until now, I had felt nothing but grief, now I found that I was happy this fight was over. I am glad that she will no longer be a threat to my unborn child. With that revelation, I looked at Keera, who was now lightly caressing my hair. "I'm ready." With those words, I helped Keera up from the floor and stood. She told me about what had happened when she escaped. Kemorte must have deliberately followed her, just so he could catch her, deliver her to my mother, and get praises. He was a twisted person; I had always thought so. He did not foresee Keera's strength and determination. I am glad I withheld the fact that she could absorb energy so expertly. He would have never allowed things to go as they had, if he had known. We walked past Kemorte's crumpled body. He will be dealt with when I get Keera to a safe place. I was unable to teleport within the Beneath, so I put Kemorte into a deep sleep until someone could retrieve him.

Keera led me down the hallway and to the stairwell. As we reached the stairs, I could hear Thena crying for help. Keera quickened her pace and I followed. We reached the cell where Thena was kneeling and banging on the invisible barrier. Keera called out, "Thena!" Thena looked up and immediately began crying, "Is it over? Can we go home now?" Keera put her hands up to the barrier, mirroring Thena's hands. "It's over. Move back so that I can break the barrier." I knew this was something Keera needed to do, so I did not make any attempts to stop her. Thena moved back as I moved behind Keera to steady her and support her with my energy. She was still weak from what she did to Kemorte and Nima, and I wanted to make sure she didn't fall and hurt herself. She closed her eyes and I could feel her focusing and reaching out to that special place she goes to in order to call upon her power. It really was amazing to see and feel her in action. Once she reached that place in her mind, it took very little work to break the energy barrier and release Thena. As if Thena had felt the energy dissipate, she ran up to Keera and held her tight. I stepped away and allowed the girls to have their moment. Thena stepped away from the hug and, speaking very loudly, "Oh my God! You are big!!! When did this happen??" Looking at me, "Raknico, you've been busy! Come here brother!" She grabbed me and gave me a very tight hug. It was foreign, but it felt warm. Moving to my ear, she whispered, "Thanks." I looked at her, a little confused, but nodded in reply. She grabbed mine and Keera's hands. "Okay, people. I don't mean to rush y'all but I kind of want to get away from my prison cell. Is it just me, or are there a lot of people talking way too loud in here?" Keera and I laughed at Thena's elevated voice. "We'll tell you all about it later." With that, we left to find the exit and the way home.

Keera

The building was like a maze. I think it took us easily a half an hour to reach a door that led to the outside. It was weird. I felt like I had been locked away for weeks, but I think we were only gone for a few days. What was most important was I had found my sister, and destroyed the people who were trying to kill me to prevent the fulfillment of the prophecy. When we did exit, it looked like a dreary fall day. The clouds broke a little and when the sunlight hit my face, I felt a sense of being home. It was so weird, because I was somewhere I had never been but I didn't feel far away from home. I let my eyes adjust to the light, then took a look around. The buildings were all destroyed. There was not much left, except the shell of what once was. It was gloomy, and it was then that I understood why this was called the Beneath. It looked like something in a bad part of town; a place corrupt with crime and somewhere you would never trust to leave your car, for fear that it would not be there when you returned. You could feel something or someone lurking around, but we did not see another soul on the streets. Nico assured me that he had an idea of how to get us back to his home. I was exhausted, so I didn't question his theories, I just followed and took in the broken scenery.

As we walked further and further away from the place of our imprisonment, I couldn't help but feel like I was back in middle school. Everyone has that school trip that they barely remember but, at the most random times, you'll get flashbacks of that day you let your school bore you to death for extra credit in class. I stopped walking and took a better look around. Raknico and Thena didn't seem to notice that I had stopped moving. *Oh, my God.* I found renewed strength and I ran up to them and grabbed Thena's arm to whirl her around. "Remember that trip we took back when I was in junior high… the furthest mom ever let us go on a school trip?" Taking a moment to think through her haze, Thena looked to the sky to try to find the memory. Her face lit up and she looked at me. "Yeah, I remember," she laughed. "You begged her because if you didn't go, you were gonna probably fail your history midterm. You couldn't afford NOT to go." She continued laughing as I pointed to the building to our left. Her eyes followed to where I was pointing and abruptly stopped laughing. "Oh, my God!... Oh.. My… GOD!" her voice kept getting louder. Nico watched the whole exchange with confusion. When Thena wouldn't stop shaking, his curiosity got the best of him. "Keera, I don't understand. What is it? What's the matter?" I didn't know any other way to explain, so I said whatever came to mind. "Nico, either your people love Earth so much that you replicated our monuments, or someone's not telling us the truth." Stepping back to look at the building in my sight, he tilted his head to get a better view. "I still don't understand. What does that old building have to do with Earth? It's nothing more than rubble on the ground. How can you even tell what it is.. eh… used to be?" I opened my mouth to speak, but closed it. This was his first time in the Beneath so he had no prior knowledge of this place. Their history is cryptic, so there isn't a way to understand why this is here. I needed more proof. I looked around and began walking. If my theory was correct, there would be more monuments around here. "Stay here with Thena for a moment. I have to check something out." I began to walk away when Nico grabbed my arm. I put my hand on top of his to reassure him. "Nico, please trust me." He reluctantly released my arm and I walked away. I don't know what I hoped to find. Whatever I find, I hope it bridges the gap in history for the Vaehte people.

Raknico

When I released Keera's arm, I felt like I was letting go of a piece of me. I knew I could trust her and I knew that she was capable of handling anything. I just worried about her in her fragile state. She walked away and got smaller and smaller the further she went. I didn't realize I was dazed until I felt Thena retreat closer to me. Thena was still in a state of shock and I did not know how to help her. I sat her down at the nearest area that looked semi-suitable for sitting. She continued to shake, but her vitals seemed to be stable. She was muttering to herself so low that I could not make out what she was saying. I bent down to listen; still nothing.

The air around us began to stir. There were people around, and they were getting closer. My heart began to beat faster. Where was Keera? Was she safe? I couldn't leave to find her because I couldn't leave Thena alone, and she was in no condition to walk. I reached out with my mind to locate Keera. The shadows began to close in. I ended my search and stood up to prepare myself for a battle. I began to receive electrical shocks when, from around the corner, I saw Keera. She was among the fallen. "Keera! Get away from them!" I began to run toward her when she put up her hands and reached into my mind. "It's okay, Nico. They're nice people." I stopped and looked around. The fallen were murmuring amongst themselves. No one was trying to hurt her. They were smiling and following her, like she was their Queen. I was always told that the fallen were cruel and unruly people. That was not the case with these Fallen, at least. I never thought this day would come, when I would be so confused about my whole existence. Keera looked past me and nodded. I turned to see Thena walking in our direction, more calm than she had been a few moments ago. Keera grabbed my hands, which made me turn to look at her. I could see the concern in her eyes. I could feel the importance of what she was about to say. "Nico, I think that... no, I am pretty sure that we are both from the planet Earth... possibly from the same country. I don't know what happened, but I think Idava would be able to help us understand more." I was at a loss for words. "Look around." I did. "Now close your eyes." I followed Keera's instructions and began to receive images. I could see children. I saw pre-teen Thena waving at me to come along. I was seeing Keera's memories. Ahead of us was a structure of a man sitting in a chair. He was made out of stone. The memory fades and she sent me an image of the ruined building in front of us. I opened my eyes and looked at it. It resembled the man in the chair, except the pillars are missing or broken and the chair and man are almost completely dust. I looked back at Keera, "How can this be?" She took my hand and led me forward, "I don't know yet, but there's more to see." She took me to many different locations. There was a wall that held the names of soldiers who died during a war... the V-et-naam war. A memorial for those who died in a Korean war. There were frozen steel figures standing for this memorial. There was a man who had a dream. She didn't know the whole speech or story, but I could see from her memories that he was a well-respected man who fought for equality among their... our? People. A grand statue was erected for him, and what's left now saddens me. We walked for some time and then we stopped. She showed me a white house. She said it was the house where the leader of the United States of America, the USA, lived with his or her family. The house was no longer standing, but pieces of the flag were still attached to a metal pole. Through her memories, I was able to see these things as they used to be. It was beautiful! I don't know what happened, but I know there is so much we need to learn about our history, and how so much beauty and history had been destroyed.

Keera

Though Raknico was apprehensive, I had to help him see the fallen as they are. Not only because they are nothing like he believes them to be, but because they saved my life.

I was afraid when I first sensed energy close by on my way to the White House. I still couldn't believe that this used to be Washington, D.C... at least that's the theory I'm sticking to. The White House ruin was coming into view when I got a wave of mixed emotions. There were people around, but I pretended not to notice. I wasn't sure what to do. I was never instructed on how to react to a group of fallen. I got close enough to the White House rubble and pretended to view it. The energy got closer and continued to grow closer to me. There was suddenly a very dark energy invading the energy field around me. I could no longer feel the fallen and their mixed emotions. All I felt was pure hatred and malice. I turned my head to the left, just in time to catch Kemorte's fist. "You could have loved me." I stumbled to the side, holding my mouth with my left hand and my belly with my right. "Did Raknico think that he could just send me to sleep and take me back to the Isle to be dealt with?" He stalked toward me and was upon me in two steps. He grabbed my hair and yanked my head backward. I yelped, then cursed myself for sounding weak. I landed against his body, feeling his breath on the side of my face and the growing arousal in his pants. "Your essence is a tasty thing to follow. I do enjoy the chase." He turned my head to face him, then attempted to push his tongue into my mouth. I cringed, turning myself away while closing my eyes as tight as I could. Kemorte tightened his grip on my hair and pulled me in closer. He brought a device close to my face. He trailed it down to my stomach, which made me tense. "Don't try anything, Keera. I want you, not your offspring." I began to panic because I didn't see this ending very well. He was ready to do something to my baby and I was powerless to stop him. I began to soften in his arms, thinking that the only way I could save me and my baby was to give Kemorte what he wanted from me. I should have waited until I gained my energy back before venturing out. *I'm sorry, Nico.*

Sensing my withdrawal, Kemorte put the device away. "That's a good girl." He brought his hand to my face and stroked my cheek. It took everything I had not to shrink away. I had all but given up when, from behind me, Kemorte began to scream. He lost his hold on me and I did not want to risk being caught again, so I ran and hid. When I felt like I had gotten a safe distance away, I checked in on my baby and sighed with relief that he was a little weakened, but okay. I looked to where Kemorte was now on his knees, covering his ears with his hands. At first I did not understand what was happening to him, but soon saw the shadows closing in. I could not tear my eyes away. I had never seen anything like this. Kemorte was screaming in pain but no other sound was heard. Blood began to run from between his fingers and his screams became as quiet as a whisper. The darkness I felt began to recede, and the mixed emotions returned. Kemorte dropped to the ground, and the darkness faded to nothing.

The shadows turned their attention to me and I just knew that it was my turn. I closed my eyes and connected to my baby. I needed extra support to help combat the fear coursing through my veins. My heartbeat drummed in my ears, just as several voices came through my mind, *Who are you? You are different. Are you the one?* I slowly opened my eyes to see a group of maybe twenty people looking at me. I stood up, taking in the faces. I spoke, using my voice, "Hi. I'm Keera. I'm Raknico, the Grandfather's son's, mate." I sounded fearful but stood strong, with my chin held high. *Did you hear? She spoke! She knows! Did she say mate? She IS the one!* An elderly man stepped forward. He looked like life hadn't been kind but he was in good spirits anyway. *You are the prophecy... You will save us!* It was a statement and not a question. I nodded.

It was amazing to meet so many people who were very much like me. Although the fallen spoke telepathically, the way they spoke and their attitude, was very Earth-like. They harnessed a larger range of emotions that made them very human, unlike the "unfallen" who focused solely on positive and uplifting emotions. My first impression of the "unfallen" was Stepford-wife perfect. I could understand Nima's apprehension to live a life based solely on positivity which is close to perfection. After meeting the Fallen, I now know that they are capable of so much more. The range of emotion seemed to give these people a reason to live. Although they were cast away, they seemed eternally happy, and not because they had to be, but because they wanted to be.

I had found everything that I had ventured out to find, and now it was time to show Raknico. I began to walk toward the direction where I had left Raknico and Thena. Without looking back, I could feel the fallen behind me, following. I stopped and turned around. "How is it that you understand when I speak? The others," I pointed above, "they do not understand my words well, or at all." It was silent and everyone was looking around, but I could tell that they were trying to determine how to answer. The same old man stepped forward. I was guessing that he was the leader of the group. "What is your name, sir?" *I am called Jules. To answer your question, we understand because we live in the Beneath.* "I don't understand." Jules turned toward the group and then back to me. He sighed. *"I know not why this is. We see things in the Beneath that they do not in The Isle. You are the first to speak in this tongue. That is how we know you are different. That is how we know you are here to save us all!"* I pondered this for a moment. It made sense that if this was Earth, or even a replication of Earth, then our language and historical elements had to be around. I walked up to Jules, "Well, I will do my best." I turned and began walking again, aware that they were still following. The gap between the group and I decreased as we got closer to the spot where I had left Raknico. By the time we rounded the corner, Jules was walking alongside of me, beaming with pure excitement.

After I showed Raknico what I had seen and what I remembered, he was stunned to say the least. He looked as though he was a six-year-old boy who had just learned that

Santa Claus wasn't real. I could understand. I had similar feelings. We thought ourselves as different species, when we may in fact be the same, yet from a different place in history. He brought his hand up to my mouth, where Kemorte had hit me. I winced, but gave him a smile as soon as I felt a change in his energy. I was too exhausted to send calming energy, so I hoped that my smile was enough. I felt a spark on my cheek and registered that the baby was attempting to help Raknico. He returned my smile and I felt his anger ebb, but the silence between us lingered. I looked to his face. "We need to find Idava. Do you think she would still meet us at the meeting place? She said she could feel us and meet us." Raknico pondered for a second before responding,

"It's worth a try." Taking Raknico's lead, we walked toward the rendezvous location. We had set this location for two reasons. The first reason was because neither Raknico or I had ever been to the Beneath, and we were informed that the way in was never the way out. The second reason was in case something went wrong, which it did, we could all come together in one place and leave together. We arrived at the meeting place. It was empty and quiet. I could feel Idava but could not locate her. We waited patiently, knowing that Idava would sense us and know to come. Moments later, up on the hill, she came into sight. Her first reaction was shock. I guess we arrived with a lot more people than she was expecting. "What is the meaning of this? Why have you brought them here?" The fallen shrieked back in fear. I couldn't understand why. Idava was speaking in a way that I didn't think was possible. She spoke out loud, in English, but also spoke in our minds in the native language. I stepped forward, ignoring her questions. "Idava, I need you to tell me... to tell us, why the Beneath feels like home. I mean, I just saw the President's house, or what was left of it. You have to know something." Idava stood silent for a moment and then took a deep breath and let it out, "Child, I have had the same feelings, but I don't know for sure. I've been to the Beneath many times. I have seen many areas of it and when I was on my mission on Earth, there were places that gave me déjà vu. I have told you that things weren't what they seemed. I spoke the truth. I just don't have a definite answer to your question. If we were able to read our history, I would be able to tell you something more. I will tell you, we are not all that different from one another and we may share a history. I see it. I have always seen it. But could never relay it to the High Appointed. It was against our whole existence." She hung her head down low. I believe this was the first time where she didn't have all the answers, as it related to the world she perceived. I walked up the hill to meet Idava. I grabbed her hand and she looked up at me, almost ashamed. "Don't worry, Idava, we will find out the truth." With that, we set off to prepare for my destiny. The fallen remained in the Beneath. I gave them an encouraging smile. No matter what we had just discovered, the new world that would be brought about in the prophecy had yet to be established, so the old rules still applied.

CHAPTER TWENTY-FIVE

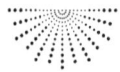

Keera

*O*ur next destination was Mount Appointed. I was hesitant, at first, because I wasn't sure I was ready to meet the group of people who were responsible for making all the decisions for these people. I mean, some of the decisions were just wrong and others I didn't understand. But I had no choice. Idava told me that the dreams Raknico and I had were due to the prophecy, and that we would have to have the baby on Mount Appointed. So, against my better judgement, I went, along with my sisters, Saniyah, Shanluk, Idava, and of course Raknico, up to Mount Appointed to meet the High Appointed. It didn't help that I still felt bad for being the one to inform Jules and his group that they had to stay in the Beneath. They were not allowed back into The Isle. Such a horrible thing to leave people behind when you know they were banished unjustly. He made me promise to come back. I told him that I was going to make things right again and if I had my way, everyone would be treated with equality and not cast aside. He gave me a smile, then opened his mouth and said thank you. It was the first time I had heard him, or any of the people here, speak. I smiled back and surprised him with a hug. When I turned away from him, I could feel the positive energy flowing from the group. I knew that I could not mess this up and I had to go back and save those people.

We arrived at Mount Appointed by late evening. I felt as if I had been up for days. I was so exhausted, I didn't care who we met, just as long as I saw a bed pretty soon. Idava brought us up to this big mansion. It was beautiful, and appeared to be floating on a cloud. The mist was thick at the foundation and a set of stone stairs appear to come up from nothing. She began to climb the large steps to the front door. She opened the heavy French doors and walked in. We all stared up at the door where Idava had disappeared. This was going to be interesting. We walked up reluctantly. There was no lock, nor a butler to meet us at the door. We walked into a grand foyer, where we met with Idava. She turned and addressed us, "This is the High Appointed's dwelling. You will be guests in this place. Please, make yourselves at home." She faced me, "Please, let me show you to your room so that you may rest. We will meet with the High Appointed tomorrow." I turned to Raknico and he looked at me, smiled, and kissed me on the forehead. I followed Idava up the stairs. The building was massive. It was as though the hallway went on and on. We walked down the hall for a minute in silence. We stopped at a room to the left. Instead of opening the door, Idava just stood there, facing the door, "I want to thank you." Thank me? Since I had asked her about the Beneath, she had been quiet and lost in her thoughts. "Thank me for what?" She sighed and turned toward me, "It may be because we both lived in your world for a time and are able to see the similarities, but I am thanking you for not making me feel crazy." She gave me a small smile before continuing, "No one believed me. Not even the Grand Father believed me when I sent my initial reports from my mission. He dismissed them, so I stopped speaking on them. So, thank you." She grabbed my hands and gave them a squeeze. She turned around and opened the door. She walked me through the room… well, suite. It was the largest room I've ever seen in a house. It was like it was a house inside of a house. We walked into the foyer, shoes clacking on the marble. It opened onto the living room. The kitchen was to the left of the living room and the study was to the right. There was a bathroom next to the study, and a winding staircase that led to the master bed and bath. The tour ended in the master bedroom. Idava seemed to be back to her normal self once she had finished the tour. She started out of the room to leave me to rest. Before she shut the door, she turned, "I've seen many versions of the future, you know? I didn't believe it, but now I'm convinced that we are on the verge of something great!" Before I could respond, she softly shut the door. Thinking nothing further, I laid on the fluffy bed, closed my eyes, and entered dreamland.

Raknico

While Idava escorted Keera to our room, I decided to take a tour of the palace. I had never been up here. Although my father is the Grand Father, and is usually invited here for meetings, it was forbidden for me to attend with him. He would always have stories about how grand this place was. He even told me of a reflecting pool called a looking glass, that was able to see whatever you wanted it to. I had my heart set on finding that looking glass. I wanted to find my father and Keera's mother. Nima would not give me answers, and there was no way that Kemorte would have cooperated and told me anything, if he hadn't expired for causing harm to Keera. It was very important that I find that glass. It was my only chance at finding my father. I opened door after door and found everything but a looking glass. There were fine furnishings, libraries, an elegant kitchen and dining room, bedrooms and suites, but nothing resembling a looking glass. I'm sure I would know the looking glass on sight. There aren't any other reflective surfaces on the whole planet, and anything like it would have to be the looking glass. Wandering around the halls, I got lost. I tried not to panic. I knew that if I exhausted all my options, I could teleport to the foyer from memory, or teleport to Keera through our bond. I continued to walk down the current hall. Because I was lost, I decided to just try to find a way back to the foyer. When I came to a dead end, I decided that I should teleport and end my search for the day. Just when I was focusing on my location, I receive a strange vibration from the room on my left. I looked through the keyhole and saw something in the middle of the room. *This had to be it.* I had never felt this level of vibration before. Without a thought, I went for the door knob, but it wouldn't budge. Locked. I knew without a doubt that this was the room that held the looking glass. I doubted that I would find a person willing to open the door and allow me to peek at the looking glass. I could try and teleport, but I am not sure this small glimpse of the room is enough to use as a focal point. I think that the only way to gain access is by approval from the High Appointed, and that was unlikely. I needed to get creative; the sooner the better.

Keera

I woke up with a start, not recognizing my surroundings. I looked around and realized where I was. I was in the bedroom of the suite in the house within the house. I felt movement next to me and froze. I looked over and it was Raknico, sound asleep. I no longer felt tired, and had the need to move around or I would get too stiff. I decided to take a walk and explore the house. It was quiet, so it had to be the dead of night. It was a perfect moment to try to get my thoughts together and get comfortable in this new place, since I don't have too much time before the baby arrives. I walked down a hall on the main floor. I marveled at the elegant marble floors that spanned throughout the entire floor. I ran my hand across the ebony wood doors and hand-painted walls. The wood was beautiful and hand-carved. The design was so intricate; whoever carved it must have had a lot of time on their hands. As I walked and thought about the time it would have taken the artist to carve the wooden frames, I came across a library. The room had wall-to-wall and floor-to-ceiling shelves of books. There were a couple of leather armchairs with matching coffee tables set up in front of a fireplace. I ran my hand along one of the walls of books. I didn't think I would find a library here. Raknico and Idava had both told me that there were no records kept, because all the people were able to pull from memories. This must be the planet's history; the last records of how the world was shaped into what it is today. At the realization, I grabbed the closest book with excitement. I blew away the dust and looked at the cover. Another fact dawned on me. The symbols I see everywhere, and on everyone's skin. This is the library that holds the history of the world, but no one can read it because they do not understand the language it is written in. I stared at the title. I tried to make sense of it, but nothing came to me. *What does this mean?* I whispered to myself. I took the book to the closest chair. It was as large as an encyclopedia volume, and just as heavy. I needed to know if this was Earth; I needed to know what happened so that the fallen could be accepted again. I opened the book. The binding cracked because it had never been opened before. I flipped page after page and the further I looked, the less it made sense. I was about to close the book when a new wave of determination hit me. I closed my eyes and randomly picked a spot on the page. "Resi. What do you mean?" I stared until my eyes blurred. Losing myself in thought, I couldn't understand what this word meant. "Some light reading to help you sleep?" I gasped and almost dropped the hefty book. I turned to see Idava at the doorway. "Oh, I woke and didn't feel tired anymore. I hope you don't mind. I just wanted to take a look around." I picked up the book from my shrinking lap and began to return it to its rightful place. "No worries, child. Something tells me that you will find value in those books where we never could." I returned to my seat with the book in hand.

She turned to leave, but I needed to tell her how I felt. "Idava..." She turned to face me. "Thank you." Idava left me to my thoughts. I sat and thought about the word I had pointed to from the book. I must have dozed off, or gone into deep meditation, because I found myself hovering over my younger self, having tea with Thena. "Ouldway ouyay ikelay oremay eatay, eerakay?" Young Thena spoke while holding up our ceramic tea kettle. I held up my cup and responded, "Ye..esyay pl..es..easeplay." I remembered that day. Thena had been speaking pig latin with her friends at school and I had been begging her for weeks to teach me. I always wanted to be just like her. She was my idol. I spent that whole morning learning the rules of pig latin. I told her I wanted to present my new way of speaking to my friends at my tea party at 2 pm. Thinking back on it now, I could only laugh because my friends consisted of my furry stuffed bunny, Gloria, my brown teddy bear with one eye, Hook, and my baby doll, Abby. I was so nervous to speak, but I'd do anything to impress Thena. I would never forget that day because that was our last tea party with that tea set. As Thena was pouring my pretend tea, my cup slipped from my hand and onto our hardwood floor, shattering into a million pieces. Mom was so upset with us, but she eventually got over it and bought us a new tea set. It was durable plastic, and not the same, so we never played with it. My memory began to fade as I heard my name being called somewhere in the distance. The world around me started to fade in. I was again in the library. The sun was beginning to come through the shutters. I was slouched over in the chair I was sitting in... a very uncomfortable position. "Keera, what are you doing in here?" I sat up and began to stretch. It was Raknico calling for me. "I had the weirdest dream. I dreamt about a tea party that Thena and I had when we were younger.

It was so funny..." I let out a little giggle, "we used to speak pig latin and--"

"Pig Lat-tin?" Raknico interrupted. I waved him off, "Oh, Pig Latin is a game children played. It's been around for a long time. It's like a secret language we used to say things around our parents that we didn't want them to underst--" I stopped mid-sentence. "I got it!" I looked around where I was sitting. I didn't remember putting the book away. I quickly got up and ran to the shelves. "Where is it? Where is it?"

"What are you looking for?" Raknico was fast behind me. "The book I was reading yesterday. Oh, forget it. I'll just pick another one. I'm sure they are written in the same language." I picked a book from the shelf, moved to the closest chair, and opened it to a middle page. My finger scanned the page. I didn't know how or why that exact memory showed up when it did. Quite frankly, that has been a theme recently. But I am thankful for the boost. I turned the outside world off and put on my mental detective hat, hoping I was going to make a great discovery today.

I must have been sitting there awhile. Someone had brought in breakfast and Idava had come in to check my and my baby's health. The room was quiet, but still hummed. "Yes! Hmmm. I need a mirror," I whispered to myself, then looked up to see who was there to assist. I was alone. I lifted the book and held it as best as I could against my chest. "Hello!" I yelled out when I entered the hallway. I looked left, then right. "Where is everyone?" I spoke quietly. I didn't want to exert too much energy so I reached out to Raknico with my mind. *Nico, where are you? I need your help.* Not even 30 seconds went by and he appeared by my side. "My darling, what is it? Are you unwell?" He grabbed my hands and began to scan my body with his mind for ailments. "No, I'm fine. I think I may have stumbled upon something. Can you help me locate a mirror?" Looking back at me, confused, "A mirror? We don't have any mirrors. Why do you need a mirror?"

"Well I think that your, our... whatever... ancestors may have liked childhood games." Raknico stared blankly at me. "Nevermind. I want to test my theory but I need a mirror... UGH!" I went back into the library, sat down, and looked back at the book, trying to will my mind to read the words on the page and understand them. Nothing. "Good afternoon, child. I hope you were able to get a break from these old books." I looked up at Idava, defeated. She came toward me. She placed her hand on my cheek and smiled. "It's time." Of course it was time. I had to go face to face with the High Appointed and listen to them tell me how glad they were that I am here, but how disappointed to see that I had befriended the Fallen. Blah, blah, blah. That was an argument I wasn't sure I could speak on and win, but I was going to stand up for myself and my beliefs, no matter what the cost.

Raknico

As we walked, I contemplated the things that were going through Keera's mind. She was unaware that I was lurking, because she was so preoccupied with the meeting with the High Appointed. She had nothing to worry about because I knew that they would love her once they saw her, and they would not think low of her for befriending the Fallen. I thought they would want to know about her thoughts on the library. They needed to understand that she was here to save them, to save us all.

It didn't take us long to get to the meeting hall. The meeting hall was the room where the High Appointed met with the people of The Isle. In this room, many fates had been determined. I had come here many times with my father, but never to be judged for any wrong actions. For some reason, I felt like today would be the day that I would find out how it felt to be judged by the High Appointed.

We walked into the meeting hall to be greeted by the silence of an empty room. "Well, where are they?" Keera looked at me expectantly. I smiled and grabbed her hand. "The High Appointed always make an entrance into a room. They will be here shortly." We took the seats that were placed in front of the altar for us. We all sat there quietly as if we were waiting for sentencing. The room began to buzz and I knew that meant the High Appointed would be in soon. We all rose to our feet. From the door to our left came five individuals in long golden robes, with hoods pulled close around their faces, shadowing their features. No one knew who the High Appointed were. The only one with an identity was the Oracle, because she was often sent on missions. All others were to be kept hidden away. No one knows how they are chosen or why this is so. It has been tradition for so long that no one even cares to question it. I was beginning to question many things. The High Appointed took their seats, which prompted us to bow. *You may sit.* This was spoken in our heads by one of the High Appointed, without indication of who had sent the message. We sat down and instinctively Keera grabbed my hand. The buzz in the room began to increase as soon as Keera and I touched. It was a mixture of our bond and the disappointment that the High Appointed felt. *I see you have not yet learned the way of our people, Keera. You continue to break our laws.* Keera's heart picked up in pace and I felt the defiance slowly building. Using her speaking voice, she defended her actions. "I'm sorry. I don't mean any disrespect. I am new to this and I just hoped that it wouldn't be too much of a problem if we connected." *You will show respect and you will follow our laws. You will learn your place.* There was a surge of power within Keera before she stood up and stepped forward. "Or what? You will cast me out for being different...like you did the fallen. Look--"

The buzz continued to rise as the High Appointed spoke, *They chose to not follow laws, as you are choosing now. You have no right-*

Keera matched their vibration. "According to *your* prophecy, I do." Keera felt she had checkmated them. *We do not need this coming from some human.* I felt the insult hit Keera hard before she spoke again. "Oh, is that what this is all about... me being human. Well, let me tell you, we may be more alike than you realize, so I'd be careful about what I said if I were you." The vibration of the room lowered when the High Appointed reacted to what was said, *What is this you speak of?* Keera looked back to Idava and me. I gave her a mental push to continue. "I was in the library and I believe I have found a way to decipher your history." The High Appointed turned toward each other and spoke their doubts. *What did she say?... She must be mistaken... A young human doing something our most promising scholars could not do?* Turning back toward us, *Have you translated any?* Keera deflated slightly. "I haven't actually translated any of it. I just have a theory." The room began to buzz again, *See, she is mistaken. The young human and her fantasies. Are we sure the prophecy is about her?* Keera was at her last ounce of will. "Look, in your world, I lack the tools I need to test my theory." *We are advanced. I am sure we have what you are looking for.* Keera rolled her eyes. "I need a mirror."

Silence.

"You know... a surface with a reflection."

Silence.

"Oh! I know you have to have a big container of water... that would do." As if the High Appointed wanted to keep the past hidden, they still sat in silence. That's when it hit me. They had probably the last remaining reflective surface on the planet, besides the container of water. This was my chance to get into that room and check out the looking glass for myself. I stood. "There is one here on Mount Appointed. I have heard of it from my father, the Grand Father." The High Appointed were not pleased with my outburst. *No one but the High Appointed is allowed to peer into the Looking Glass. It is against the laws.* "What about your history? Isn't it worth it to find out about the centuries before you?" Keera tried to plead her case. There was a long-drawn-out silence. *We will have to deliberate before making a final decision.* The room began to buzz again, signaling the High Appointed's departure. We all bowed. I hoped this wasn't the end of the road. Knowing the High Appointed, they had already decided, and not in our favor. Whatever we were going to do, I hoped we did it soon, because I felt like we were running out of time.

Keera

I just could not believe the High Appointed. They were nothing more than a bunch of robed nobodies that clung close to their traditions and laws. What was the point of my being here, if not to change their way of life and make it better for everyone? Doing that meant changing the laws. I went over to Raknico and felt the comfort of his arms around me. I didn't care what the High Appointed snobby group said, I craved and needed physical contact. I looked at Idava. "I don't like that group. They are hiding something. Did you see how they acted like they didn't know what a mirror was? They have one right under their nose. I understand that the laws are sacred, but what about their history? I just feel like they should have been more accommodating." I thought that was also strange, that they were most concerned about me wanting to see the Looking Glass, and not so much about me befriending the fallen. Idava approached me and grabbed my hand. "Child, you have no idea! Why do you think I was so eager to go on that mission and be away from my home for as long as I have?" We shared a laugh. "No worries, child. I will get you into that room to glance at the Looking Glass." Idava smiled at me, but I couldn't return the gesture. "Idava, what about the laws? What will happen to you if they find out?" She gave a low chuckle, "Oh, they will know as soon as it happens. You just make sure you're right."

CHAPTER TWENTY-SIX

Keera

*A*s we walked down the corridor in the dark, I couldn't seem to think about anything but failing. I don't even think it was me who was making my feet move. After the meeting with the High Appointed, Idava took us to the library to grab some of the books. She said that there was no time to waste. The moment the High Appointed gave us their answer, which we already knew would be 'no', they were going to shut down the Sacred Looking Glass room to prevent things like what we were about to do. So, with arms full of books, Idava shuffled Raknico and I down multiple corridors until we reached a door that, to me, seemed like an ordinary door. "Is this it?" I was in disbelief. It was nothing special. Like always, Idava rolled her eyes, and sucked air through her teeth before responding, "Things are never what they seem, child." She walked up to the door and closed her eyes. Within a few moments, the door unlocked. "How did you do that!" Idava continued to amaze me. "It's a mental combination lock. Only the High Appointed and the Grand Father are given the combination. I'm just glad that they haven't decided to change it in all this time. Come on, let's test your theory."

Idava pushed the door open, pulled us in, and shut the door. I looked around. It was magnificent. The floor was the most beautiful marble I had ever seen and since being here, I've seen many. The walls were made of another beautiful stone that reminded me of pure Ivory. There were openings on two of the walls that were glassless windows. The view overlooked a mountainous city. The eye-catcher in the room was the Looking Glass. It was in the center of the room and was lined with diamonds and other precious gems. It sparkled, and the vibrations of the stones beckoned me to move closer. Idava began to speak, but I couldn't hear her over the glistening in the center of the room. I couldn't fight it, so I moved closer until I was touching the rim of the looking glass. I looked in and got lost in my reflection. The image began to ripple and change. It was the beneath. I was back to my pre-pregnancy size and Raknico and I were instructing on the rebuild. I felt nothing but happiness around me. I took a good look around. Idava was there and was approaching me. She stopped right in front of me, "Child, you need to stop daydreaming and complete the task at hand. We need to get one thing done at a time, in order to see the future unfold." I jerked back into the present and saw that I was still in the Looking Glass room. Idava and Raknico hadn't noticed that I had looked into the glass. It was bizarre how it felt like I was looking into the future, yet the future Idava was speaking to me about our current predicament.

"The books! Right!" Although I spoke out loud, no one seemed to notice. I pulled the book I was carrying to my hands and opened it to a page that looked like it would be a good test page. I held the book up over the Looking Glass and waited until the reflection of the book stopped rippling. To my surprise, the image never cleared. Instead, a new image appeared. It was a lab. Everything was wrong. It was like a bomb went off and I could hear people in the distance. It almost sounded like everyone was running around with their heads cut off. The sound was playing in my mind like I had on a pair of headphones. There was a scientist at a desk, looking at results. He didn't seem happy. He got up and walked away with his head down. The image clouded and when it cleared, that same scientist was at a home shouting for someone named Marie to hurry up and pack. A woman appeared, a very pregnant woman, in the doorway. "I'm ready." She carried a small suitcase in her hand and had tears in her eyes. "Marie, don't worry. I will get you out. I will get you somewhere safe so that our son can grow up safe and away from here."

"I'm scared, Ronald." He took her into a hug. I heard his thoughts as he grabbed the suitcases and began to walk to a car. *I should have never included myself in the experiments. How am I ever going to tell Marie that I can't go with her. She will be heartbroken. But I have to do it! I want my son to have a life outside of captivity. If they ever found out Marie was pregnant, they would try to take her and I can't allow it. I WON'T allow it.* As he loaded the car, I got a glimpse of his side. He had writing tattooed on him. Similar to Raknico's but before they disappeared, I noticed that they were in English. Another image appeared, and Ronald was driving in a high-speed chase. Marie was in the passenger seat, far into labor, and there was a line of cars in pursuit. Ronald managed to shake the line of cars and found a cave. Marie was in so much pain. She kept telling him she was ready to push. I instinctively wrapped my arms around my stomach. After the groaning and moaning, she finally pushed out a baby boy. The baby let out a loud wail but when Ronald began to speak to him in his mind, the baby stopped crying and looked to his father. It was as if he knew what Ronald was saying. Ronald examined his son. He was a healthy baby boy, but something was different. His skin was darker than both his pale-skinned parents, and he had words and symbols. "He is amazing, Marie!" he said, speaking to his wife. "Unbelievable!" Speaking to himself, "It's like his skin understands hexadecimal, or some other computer representation." He gave his son to his mother. Marie looked at their son and her smile faded. She looked at Ronald questioningly, with concern in her eyes. "What's wrong with him? Why does he look like this? His eyes; the color wavers." Ronald sighed. There was no time like the present. "Marie, honey? My body has been affected by the experiments at the lab. I don't know for how long, but my theory is that, whatever was absorbed into my body also affected our son when he was conceived." He closed his eyes, expecting her to be angry. "Is that why we are running away?" He looked up at her and grabbed her free hand. "Yes. No one knew you were pregnant. I purposefully kept it a secret because I wasn't sure if our child might also be affected. It gets worse. Whatever we were experimenting with has become airborne. I need to get you as far away as possible. I'm taking you out to our family ranch. My sister will meet us there and we will live away from society as long as possible. I think we will--." Before he could finish, he heard thoughts concerning finding the scientist needed in questioning. Ronald knew all too well what that meant. He turned to Marie, "We have to go. They're here." Marie began to protest but was wrapped up with their son in hand and carried in the opposite direction of the cave's entrance. When they reached the car, a sense of dread hit him. Ronald ushered Marie into the driver's seat. She looked around in confusion, "Wait, what are you doing?" Ronald hurriedly looked around, "Marie, you have to take our son and get to that ranch. I will meet you there." He bent over to the small face in Marie's arms. Projecting his thoughts instead of thinking, *"Young one, you must tell our story. You carry our history with you and you must ensure that these experiments are not forgotten, and our mistakes may be reversed."* He took his son into his arms. "Marie, what will we name him?" Marie wiped a tear from her eye, "Noah. I've always liked Noah." Ronald smiled, "I like that." He looked at his son. "Noah, protect your mom. I will be with you both soon." He placed the baby in the passenger's seat, then returned to the driver's door. He took Marie in his arms and gave her a kiss. They both cried. Ronald searched Marie's eyes. "I will meet you there. I need to make sure no one follows you, first. Get to the ranch and stay there. Here," he placed a computer memory card in her hand. "This has all the experiment data on it. Keep it safe." Marie whispered, "I love you." Ronald didn't trust himself to speak, so he let go and turned away. Marie watched him for a moment then got into the car and drove away. Ronald spoke to her in her mind, hoping she would hear, *I love you, Marie. I will always love you.*

The image disappeared, and the reflection of the pages appeared. As I stared at the pages, I didn't even realize that Idava and Raknico had joined me. Raknico wiped away a tear I didn't know was on my cheek. He spoke in my mind, *"What happened?"* I looked at him, confused. "You didn't see any of that?" Idava looked at me, perplexed, "What happened? What did you see? You have been staring into the Looking glass, at the book's reflection, for some time." I looked back at the book's reflection and my confirmation hit me. The words began to make sense to me. I looked at Raknico, "Look, I can read this! I have to read very slowly because I have to rearrange some of the letters, but this is English." We grabbed each other and jumped for joy. Our celebration was short-lived because the High Appointed sent guards to the room. I didn't even think that guards existed, but there they were, in their armor suits, similar to the flight suits Raknico and his crew wore. "You are in a forbidden area. Come quietly or we will detain you." Idava stepped forward and placed herself in front of Raknico and I. "We will come quietly, but we would also like an audience with the High Appointed. We have information that is pertinent to the survival of our kind."

Raknico

Everything was happening too fast. The Looking Glass was within my reach and I was still unable to use it to locate my father. Keera saw something in the looking glass, something monumental, but didn't get a chance to tell us about it because of the Appointed's guards. I saw a few clips in her mind, but they were going so fast that I couldn't understand the meaning. I guess the most important takeaway from this was that Keera, brilliant as she is, had solved the mystery behind our history. I couldn't believe that the prophecy was coming true. Now, if I could only find my father.

We arrived back at the meeting room to wait for the High Appointed to arrive. This was going to be a very interesting meeting. The High Appointed would want to punish us for breaking into the Looking Glass room and Keera would want to give the detailed account of what she had witnessed by looking into the forbidden Looking Glass. I hoped that what Keera had to divulge would be enough for the High Appointed to forgive our little break-in. I just wish I knew how this would pan out. The air around us began to hum. The High Appointed were close by. They entered the room swiftly and smoothly, as if they were floating. They took their chairs and silenced their energy. Their posture and lack of energy revealed nothing of what was destined to happen. We waited and waited for something, anything, to happen. I could feel Keera's impatience growing. She wanted to tell us all what she had witnessed but didn't want to appear rude and defiant. The energy she gave off was so much like an itch you could not reach to scratch. She reached her tipping point and before I could grab her head or tell her not to speak, she spoke with speed, "Ok, I know we were forbidden to go to the Looking Glass, but you need to know what I saw when I tested my theory... which, by the way, I proved." *SILENCE!*

The room began to vibrate as the High Appointed spoke aloud and in unison. *You will not speak again. You are disobedi--.* Their voices were cut off in a choke. I could feel their power moving closer to us and disappearing. I reached out to Keera, but she had her eyes shut and her hands balled into tight fists at her side. I looked into her mind and the High Appointed's power was coming to her. She was absorbing it. The power was too much for me, so I retreated from her mind. As if she was taking in too much, Keera doubled over and put her hand to her stomach. Something was happening to Keera and the baby. I grabbed Keera and let her fall into me. "Raknico, am... I... dying?" Her voice came out in breathless whispers. I looked into her eyes and wiped her tears. "I don't know what's happening, but I will not let you die." I sat on the floor with Keera's head in my lap. I turned to Idava, who was instructing the Appointed guards. The guards left the room and Idava turned and looked at me with joy in her eyes. "She's in labor, Raknico. She is where she needs to be. Don't worry too much."

The Appointed guards came back into the room with towels, water, and the medical bag we brought from our journey back to my world. I watched as Idava took various medical tools out of the bag. There were many sharp objects that I'd never seen before. She must have seen my wide eyes. "Raknico, remember your primary school lessons?" I nodded. "Remember your history. Remember your culture. Women are meant to have babies. The High Appointed makes the decisions on who should be born or reborn, then, after a time, the woman who carries the baby, releases the baby from her body." I nodded again. "A baby of our kind reaches out for energy to assist the mother in an easy delivery. That is why our births are 100% successful, and also why they are virtually painless." I nodded yet again. She brought her hands to my chin and lifted my head so that my eyes would meet her eyes.

"This child requires special energy. That is why we needed to be here with the High Appointed. But because Keera is not quite one of our kind, I don't know what to expect from her delivery. What I need you to do is reach out to heal her and make her comfortable. She will make it. I promise you that." With that last statement, Idava went back to preparing for the worst possible early human birth.

Keera was moaning and groaning so loud, and her pain was so intense, that I felt it through our bond. I was so lost in the pain that I temporarily forgot that I could heal her pain. I closed my eyes and tried to make her feel at ease. There was so much energy that I was having trouble focusing. She quieted down and in the distance, I could hear Idava encouraging me to help, and encouraging Keera to remain calm. I felt surrounding energies assisting in the greatest birth our people would ever see. I just hoped that she didn't have to suffer too much longer. I was about to become a father. All I could think at that moment was of Keera, and how I wished my father was here to witness.

Keera

"Mommy, I just want my mommy."

I grit the words through my teeth. Even with Raknico trying to take my pain away, it's the residual pain that lingers in my spine. I feel like I am about to die, but I hear Idava tell me that I'm actually about to have a baby. Why do women do this time and time again? I thought having a baby was supposed to be a joyous time. All I want to do is rip him out. It was weird how the baby started taking energy from the High

Appointed. The energy was too much for me to bear, but somehow, I withstood it. The energy felt like it had a purpose, but because it couldn't find an entryway, it leaves just as it comes into me. So much pain in the past few hours... or has it been days? I don't even know how much time has passed but I feel so much pressure. I'm so tired but I know I have to keep moving on, if only to tell everyone what I saw in the Looking Glass. The pressure is building again. "I... think. I'm ready." The pressure increases with each contraction and the desire to push is almost impossible to ignore. "I'm ready! Idava, I'm ready." *Get this baby out of me!!!* Raknico tries to soothe me in my mind but I think I've gone hysterical because I shut him down every time he reaches out. From somewhere in the room, I hear Idava instructing me, "Alright, child, push... that's right, push now." I give into the urge to push and I push with all I have. I can't breathe but I keep going. Push. Push. Push. Breathe. Breathe. Breathe. Push. Push. Push. "Almost finished. I see the head." Idava updates me on my progress. I feel Raknico's joy permeating through my bones and it gives me the strength to keep going. Push. Breathe. Push. Breathe. Push. Breathe. Then, like the world stopped moving, I hear the most beautiful sound I've ever heard: the cry of my baby.

"It's a boy!" Idava announces to the room. Raknico's joy is uncontainable and I hear him speak in my mind, *A boy! You did it, Keera! I love you. You are amazing!* He continues with the high praises, but I feel like something is wrong. Sensing my concern, Raknico alerts Idava. "Idava, something's not right. You promised me!" Idava rushed to my side and I opened my eyes. "Child, what's wrong? What is it?" Barely able to speak, I respond in a whisper, "So much pressure. The energy is rising." Idava closes her eyes, then opens them and smiles. She leaves my side to get back into position. "Okay, child. It's all part of the process. Get ready to push again." Not done!? There's more to having a baby? I have no strength to speak while I prepare myself for more. Raknico was in full panic-mode and was not helping with the pain. I reach out to him and grab his hand. "Raknico, I am meant to survive. We can do this." I am unsure if I am telling the truth, but I need him to be with me so that I can at least try and make it. He seems to find strength in my words and went back to relieving my pain. I felt the pressure build again, and the need to push increase. Letting the room disappear, I focus. Push. Breathe. Push. Breathe. Push. Breathe. I relax for a moment to try and catch my breath. Before I could even gasp for my next breath, it was time to push again. Push. Breathe. Push. Breathe. Push. Breathe. My body relaxes and I smile, before the world goes black.

CHAPTER TWENTY-SEVEN

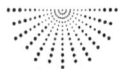

*W*ith the birth complete and the prophecy falling into place, it was as if the world ceased to exist. Everything was still. The Vaehte people did not emit energy, nor did they use their minds for anything but internal wonderment. It was only a moment, but in that moment, so many things occurred. Everything was unclear: the true meaning of the prophecy, the fate of the Isle, the fate of the people, and the destiny of those carrying out the prophecy. The Vaehte people knew that if the world went dark, there would be no light energy available on the whole planet and it would cease to be.

In that moment, a trembling wave of energy erupted from the top of Mount Appointed. All eyes fell to the energy wave as fear and excitement grew in all the people of Vaehte. The High Appointed, witnesses to the birth, were in awe and filled with anxiety for what was to come. After the prophetic birth, the draining of the High Appointed's energy ceased and released them from their paralyzing hold, yet they still stood motionless from shock. They fear the power that will result from this birth. They have never come across any being that could paralyze them, and had the ability to siphon the power reserve that only the High Appointed could possess and distribute. So small, yet so powerful against the High Appointed already. The ground began to tremble and hum. The people of Vaehte reached panic mode and looked for shelter. As disaster broke out all around, the sound of infant cries could be heard from everywhere. The hidden gateways to the Beneath arose and opened, no longer resembling a prison.

In the High Appointed meeting room, Idava and Raknico tried, with everything they had, to revive Keera. She had stopped breathing right before the disaster started. Although the energy in the room was stricken with grief, and chaos broke out across The Isle, The High Appointed stayed composed. If the pain and suffering outside wasn't heard, they would have never known something was completely wrong. The only sound heard in the room was Idava saying, "Clear" when she used the defibrillator to try to jump start Keera's heart. When it seemed like the electricity would not wake her, Raknico knelt closer to Keera's head, trying to will her awake with his mind. He no longer felt their bond, and now his heart held a hole that would never be refilled.

Idava stepped back from Keera, so that the little family could touch and say their final goodbyes. Raknico closed her eyes and continued to shed tears. He stroked her cheek, that was now a little cooler than it was a moment ago. Keera was meant to survive and help rebuild the world. Raknico could no longer handle the grief, so he got up and started walking away from his future. First his mother left him, and now Keera was leaving him, too. He could not see the point in living without Keera.

Raknico screeched to a halt and dropped down to his knees, as if he were being electrocuted in short bursts. He turned and looked at Keera. A little hand stretched out and was grazing Keera's cooling body. He reached out, but still did not feel their bond. He didn't have the strength to understand what had happened, so he began to turn, to retreat again. The little hand flailed again, hitting Keera's body, causing Raknico to shriek this time. He reached toward Keera, looking at her slack face. He noticed the infant's hand waving about, and every time it came into contact with Keera, he felt a little energy shock that reminded him of when he had first met his mate. He crawled to her side, speaking urgently in his mind, *Keera, can you hear me? Stay with me; we need you; come back to me.* With each swipe of the little hand, Raknico welcomed the electrical shock. The room watched in wonder as the little family fought to stay together. Without notice, the chaos outside ceased and all was quiet yet again. No one spoke, thought, or moved, in fear of what could come next. Raknico continued to reach out to Keera. He felt a hint of their bond return, just slightly, although she still was not breathing. He kept watch over Keera for any signs of life. He didn't care if it took days, he had a small hope that she would return to him. He bundled the wailing infant in his hands, handing him to Idava. As if the world moved in slow motion, Keera sprang forward and gasped for air. The air around us went back to normal, with the buzzing of everyone's energy cycling through. Outside, you could hear thunderous celebrations breaking out with joy of Keera's return. Keera opened her eyes to everyone looking down at her, waiting for something to happen. Her throat felt dry and her body felt like it had been hit by a truck. She leaned into Raknico and said the first thing that came to mind, "Where's my baby?" Her voice came out like sandpaper scraping against itself. Raknico smiled and leaned down to kiss her. Idava held out a glass of water. "I think you should try this first." Lifting a shaky hand, she grasped for the cup. Seeing the weakness, Raknico assisted by lifting her head with one hand, and holding the glass with the other. She drank swiftly in anticipation of seeing her son for the first time. Idava reached into the bassinet and retrieved a small infant. With the contentment of a grandmother, she handed the infant to Keera. "He's a tender one." Holding him in her arms, touching his chubby cheek, Keera wept. She whispered to him how grateful she was for him, and he snuggled close to her like he understood what she was saying. "And this one is willful." Idava reached in and retrieved another small infant. Keera looked at Raknico, bewildered. Raknico spoke with quiet eagerness. "They're twins! We have a boy and a girl." He could not contain the excitement as he helped Keera position both babies in her arms. Keera looked at her baby girl and she looked back at her, almost as if to say: 'I found you.' It was at that moment when Keera realized that it was her baby girl's determination that brought her back from where she was headed. She snuggled her baby girl and whispered thank you. She brought both babies closer and wept tears of joy.

EPILOGUE

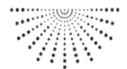

6 Months later...

Raknico

I am still in disbelief at how much my existence has changed. Not too long ago, I thought my world was falling away, but my Keera came back to me and our children. We have taken up residence in the High Appointed Palace, which may not be just for the High Appointed for long, so that we can be close to what's left of our history. Keera is sitting in a rocker chair, with both our little ones on her lap, slowly falling asleep to the sound of her voice. I am thoroughly enjoying our time, but in the back of my mind, I can't help but shake the need to locate Grand Father. I have waited these six months, giving Keera time to heal and nurture our children, but I have some fear that the longer we wait, the harder it will be to locate Keera's mother and The Grand Father. Keera revealed what she saw in the looking glass, which turns out that we are more alike than different, so she has been splitting her time with our children and the Looking Glass library, reading and searching for answers. I am determined that tonight I will raise the question, in hopes that she is ready to share what she has found in the Looking Glass library and move forward with our rescue mission.

Keera

I still can't believe I am a mother. I look down at these sleeping faces and fall in love all over again. Raknico has been very encouraging and the best emotional support I could ever imagine. Thena and Mara are very supportive and help me, but I miss my mother so much and really need her by my side. I know Raknico can feel my sadness sometimes, but it is my children, Orion and Carina, who are my center and who give me hope that I will be joined again with my parents. Raknico is growing impatient with the progress, but after spending the day in the Looking Glass library, I think I finally have a lead on where my father and mother may be located. I get up and place the twins in their crib. I stand there and watch as Carina and Orion sleep before stretching and walking out. I can feel Raknico in our living area, so I follow his energy with gladness. He turns around as I approach, sensing my joy. I look into his eyes, sending the most joyous energy before speaking. "Nico, I've found them." I sit down and Raknico wraps me in his arms. We've come so far since our first meeting, when he was just Mr. Gorgeous and I was just some annoying, yet mysterious, "human". We take this moment to absorb and enjoy each other's energy. We allow the moment to continue as our living space begins to fill with luminous jubilation. Such an intimate moment that I want to hold on to forever, but I know that we have work to do. No matter what is to come next, we know that, together, we will succeed.

The End.

MEANWHILE...

Terafey and Susan sat cuddled up on a couch in a low-lit living room. The room was silent, as they both were so far into their own thoughts. Susan's panic began to seep out into the room's energy. Terafey turned so that they could meet eye to eye, "Susan, they will find us. Do you trust me?" A single tear falls from Susan's left eye, "Yes, Fey. I trust you completely. I just wish my little girls weren't alone, fighting this battle. I just hope they aren't too afraid." She began to silently weep. Terafey, who had been rubbing her arm, gave Susan's arms a squeeze. "My heart, I have prepared Keera enough to set things in motion. The prophecy will be fulfilled and when it is, they will find us. I left clues, so we won't be stuck in this time for long." The couple again sat in silence, with renewed strength and hope.

ACKNOWLEDGMENTS

I have to give a huge shout out to my sister Theia. She doesn't know how her comments about this story have positively affected my motivation to get this out into the public domain. This story is one that I am most proud of. It came to me in a dream and flowed out of my spirit. Thank you for believing in my creativity, Dee.

Jacci, thank you for pushing me to shine. I would have never had the courage to go for this on my own if not for your love and encouragement.

Mariah, of course, I look to you for inspiration. You are an established artist and I definitely want to be like you when I grow up!

Dave, you support in me everything that I do. I cannot thank you enough for the love and devotion you give me.

This story is my baby. It has given me the motivation to go through all the steps in self-publishing. I began establishing my tribe because of this story. I found Destiny and she was able to design a cover that I am proud to display for this story.

I also found Tamra who helped make this story flow and make sense to the world without taking away my voice.

If no one reads my story, I will still be proud of the progress I've made towards sharing my creativity with the world. My dreams are large and my impact may be minimal but my smile never wavers.

ABOUT THE AUTHOR

Jen Tyes is a Scrum Master at Travelers Insurance and the author of *Not This Time*. When she isn't baking or reading a gripping novel, she can be found watching horror films, hoping for a real scare. After years as a technical writer and subsequently publishing her debut paranormal novel, Jen switched gears to focus on writing speculative and horror fiction. Inspired by her favorite author, Jodi Picoult, she is also an advocate through her blog, www.aim4equanimity.com. Jen lives in Connecticut with her husband and two children. Look for her on social media.